W9-BZM-881
RECEIVED
NOV 01 2010
By

The Beginner's Guide to Living

The Beginner's Guide to Living

LIA HILLS

FSG | New York

First published in Australia by Text Publishing, 2009
Printed in August 2010 in the United States of America by RR Donnelley & Sons Company, Harrisonburg, Virginia
Designed by tk
First American edition, 2010
10 9 8 7 6 5 4 3 2 1

www.fsgteen.com

All photographs in the book were taken by Lia Hills.
"They see sky and remember what they are" on page 164 is from the television show *Firefly*, episode called "Safe."
"That's not just incense" on page 165 is from the movie *Serenity*.

Library of Congress Cataloging-in-Publication Data
Hills, Lia.
The beginner's guide to living / Lia Hills.— 1st American ed.
p. cm.
Summary: Struggling to cope with his mother's sudden death and growing feelings of isolation from his father and brother, seventeen-year-old Will turns to philosophy for answers to life's biggest questions, while finding some solace in a new love.
ISBN: 978-0-374-30659-5
[1. Grief—Fiction. 2. Interpersonal relations—Fiction. 3. Self-actualization (Psychology)—Fiction. 4. Photography—Fiction. 5. High schools—Fiction. 6. Schools—Fiction.] I. Title.

PZ7.H5635Beg 2010
[Fic]—dc22

2009019248

FOR MY BOYS

ONE

RIP

SHE LOOKS GOOD FOR A CORPSE. Except she never wore green eye shadow, was never this still. Her rib cage has been cracked open—you can't see anything, it's all been cleaned up, but I can imagine them beneath her dress, the tracks of stitches that will never heal. Some doctor thrust his hand inside her chest, reached in and touched her heart. It must affect your view of love. It didn't work, of course—her heart refused to obey his hands. Bit senseless, my dad reckoned, breaking her open when there was no longer a chance. But it's worth it, isn't it?

Her face is the wrong color, too pink, like she's stepped out of the bath, and the coffin's not her style. Especially the handles. She wore silver, not gold. Nobody else seems to have noticed—nobody's seeing anything; it's as if they're wading through syrup. Have forgotten how to be real.

I was hanging out with my friend Seb while it was happening, all that wrestling to save a life. Four days ago, that's all it's been. We were listening to music. Radiohead. Could've been worse, I guess, more disrespectful—could've been watching reality TV, or downloading porn. The problem is, I didn't feel it. I've tried, these last few days, to imagine that I sensed something, anything, the moment she left: a stab of pain, some kind of vision. But I didn't. I felt nothing last Thursday afternoon, September 1st, at 4:27, the instant that Anna Ellis, my mother, died.

Body lowered into the ground. Vigilant sparrows. Spring rain. Mud.

I feel nothing, taste nothing, not even these chocolate éclairs. Aunty Rachel, my mom's sister, made them because she knows they're my favorite, but the icing's a paste sticking my tongue to the roof of my mouth. Aunty Rachel's standing over by the open window in our living room, leaning into her brother, my uncle Carl, the curtains billowing around them like protective sails.

An old woman's staring at me but I don't know who she is. She frowns as I spit the éclair into my hand and take a look at it—hey, if people can tell fortunes from cats' guts—and thrusts a napkin in my face.

This is not right. There are people I don't know at my mother's wake.

"Hello, Will," she says. Her hair is the color of smokers' fingers. "I'm your great-aunt," she whispers too close.

"Joy," she's saying in my face, like an insult, and I want to say, *Fuck off, Joy, what a stupid name to have at a wake.* But Dad's not far away, leaning into the living room wall like it's the only thing that will hold him up, his suit all corrugated with grief.

"Joy," she says once more to test me, and "The Lord moves in mysterious ways."

I step back, but there's someone behind, hedging me in. "This is Faith," says Joy. "She's your great-aunt too."

Faith grips my arm. Her hair has the same kind of stain. "My, haven't you grown. You must be at least eighteen."

"Seventeen," I correct.

Fingertips in my bicep, she murmurs, "Anna's safe now."

I jerk away from her—it's easy, she's so small; they both are, these witches. They're the kind of sad old ladies who skulk around other people's deaths in preparation for their own.

"Safe now?" I ask, full of jagged rib cages and last thoughts, as a car steered by a drunk driver smashes into her life. Safe as houses? Safe as death?

God, Mom, where are you? Are you disappointed I'm crap at all this? You never told me what to do when you died, but you should've, because it's the only thing we can be sure of. Death gets all of us in the end. And then I see her, this girl, in the light by the window, long hair, eternal legs, generous smile she's trying to hold on to as she talks to my dad. She looks about my age and she's in a white dress—didn't anyone tell her you're meant to wear black to a wake? She touches her fingers to her lips and suddenly, I can taste chocolate, like a betrayal. I am the king of bad timing. Only a monster could think of love.

Dream.

Hags around a cauldron. One drops in eye of newt and hemlock as the other one stirs. Steam rises from the potion and forms question marks in the sky. The witches are wearing black T-shirts, one saying *Joy*, the other *Faith*. They have hair the color of a bruise and they're pointing at an angel, its wings in full flight. An angel with that girl's face. The one who wore white to a wake.

* * *

"Will?"

It's Adam. He's looming over me, smelling of airports. I stretch my legs against the sheet, and my feet touch the end of the bed.

"Hey," I say, my eyes struggling to meet the world and my brother's face. He's tanned and his hair is even shorter than when I saw him last. Must have been six months ago—he was standing next to Mom, waving as he climbed into her car, heading for the airport to fly to Malaysia, and now he's sitting on the edge of my bed. "You didn't make it."

"I tried, but I couldn't get a flight."

My mouth tastes of doubt. Adam always gets what he wants, including seats on fully booked flights. His phone rings, the theme to the *X-Men*—he digs it out of his jacket and turns it off. "So, how was it?"

"Weird." I close my eyes again. All I can see is that girl, white wings and her white dress.

"I spoke to Dad on the phone. He said Nan organized the whole thing, wake and all, bloody Catholics. How's Dad anyway? Is he all right?"

"How can you tell?"

"Good point."

Dad leaned against our living room wall all yesterday afternoon at the wake and let people come to him. He never said a word to me the whole frigging time except *Your mom would've liked those flowers*. Twenty-four years they were married—was that the best he could do?

As Adam leans on my bed, his hand lands on the open copy of *Macbeth*, which I'm studying in Lit. "Are you okay?"

"I'm in love," I hear myself saying, the words spilling into the gap between us. He looks at me sideways, and there's something about the curve of his jaw, the hazel of his eyes—I get a jolt of Mom in that casket, green eye shadow, leering great-aunts, a sensation of shrinking away from my skin. I swallow hard. "Anyway, how's okay meant to feel?"

"Jesus, I don't know. Keep expecting her to walk in that door and ask me how my flight was."

"How was your flight?"

"Smart-ass." He's shaking his head, like a fly's trying to land on it. "Long. Boring. I kept thinking about . . ."

"What?"

"Doesn't matter."

He slumps forward, all six feet of him, and stares at the floor, at a stack of books, or maybe at nothing.

I feel him shift on the edge of the bed, the aftershock. "You know, she never once talked to me about dying."

"Don't be so frigging morbid, Will."

"I'm not. I just meant . . . I don't know."

Adam's shoulders roll forward as he prepares to leave. The sleeve of his jacket is ripped.

"That's not true," I say. "I'm pissed off."

"Fair enough."

There's agreement in my brother's face but not the kind that I seek. "I mean I'm pissed off because nobody talks about what matters, not even when someone dies."

"As if that would help."

"I think it could."

Adam's shaking his head. "Still the same old Will."

"So?"

I turn away from him. I don't need this right now—Adam bringing his version of me in here, using it to hem me in. A six-year head start doesn't give him a monopoly on the truth.

"You want to know what matters, Will? It's this." He shoves his hand in his pocket and pulls out a wad of foreign notes, Malaysian I guess. He's unmoving above me except for his fist that clings to the fan of money, and I figure he's got to be joking as we focus on it, both of us held by its spell, its damp, used odor. Beyond it, my brother's face begins to loosen. "It was a shitty flight," he says, chucking the money on the bed. "I'm going to get some breakfast, see if Dad's up. You coming?"

"No."

I roll back over toward the wall. I want him out of here. There's no space for him, for anything, except this throbbing. A thick cord of grief winding itself around me.

I pull out a notebook I keep under my bed in the old wooden box my granddad gave me when I was little, before he died. He kept old postcards in it, of palm trees and deserts from the Second World War. One day he took them out to the garage and dumped them all into the recycling bin. When he was finished, he handed the box to me and said, "Keep something useful in this, more useful than these."

On a clean page in my notebook, I write what Macbeth says at the end of the play, when he finds out his wife has died: *Life's but a walking shadow . . . a tale told by an idiot, full of sound and fury, signifying nothing.*

Night collapses on the sixth day. The house is silent. Dad and Adam have gone to buy pizza—Mom was the one who cooked.

The only meal Dad can do is a roast, but we've already had that twice since she died.

I have lived six days beyond my mother.

I want to smell her. I go into my parents' room, Michael and Anna's room. Her scent is more concentrated in here than anywhere else in the house. The room is unaltered from what I can see as I lie on their bed, the bed where they made me—they don't seem the type to do it in the kitchen. These are not the thoughts I came in here for. On her bedside table is a book, maybe the last she ever read. It's called *Meditations* by Marcus Aurelius and there's a bookmark stuck in a page where some of the sentences are underlined. One of them is stark as a premonition: *All of us are creatures of a day; the rememberer and the remembered alike.*

I close the book and shroud myself in their duvet, my head on the pillow, on her side. As I inhale her I sift through the mix for nameable smells—vanilla, paper cases peeled off muffins, the generic scent of soap—my nose dislodging a hair, the red of old blood. I wind it around my finger till it begins to turn the end purple. Tough stuff, hair. I jump up and go over to their closet where all her clothes are still hanging and plunge my face into them, but I don't cry. Not even when that blue dress slips from its hanger, the dress she loved wearing to the beach, the one that made her merge with the sky. I tuck it under my arm, unhook the white plastic hanger, and snap it clean in half like a wishbone.

The crumpled duvet gives the dress shape, a body, different from hers, as I lay it out on the bed and return to the closet. I used to hide in here when I was small, it's deep enough to forget who you are. And next to a box of tangled scarves I find what I came for, at least it seems that way as I cradle it in my hands.

My mother's camera.

She taught me how to use it as soon as she was sure I wouldn't drop it, though she'd always hover and make me wear the strap around my neck. Of course I did drop it, once. At the zoo. She gasped, and for a second I saw her, this woman who loved her camera; and then the moment was gone, she was my mother once more. It was ages before she trusted me with it again.

Her Canon AE-1 SLR.

I stroke the dent next to the case clip, the dent that I made, and I feel the camera's familiar weight. I know she'd want me to have it but I can't ask. Dad might say no. He might return it to the back of the closet—whether he's capable of this, I can't be sure. I look through the viewfinder at my parents' room, at its smallness, everything leaning in on itself through the lens. His and her side of the bed. My finger hurts as I grip the body of the camera, so I unwind the hair; it curls into a question mark on my mother's pillow and leaves a lacing of white dents on my skin. I go to take a picture of it—there's still enough sun coming in through the window, my mother always preferred natural light—but I can't see the hair through the lens. It's as if it doesn't exist at all.

The front door bangs open. My brother's voice. I grab the dress and the camera and head for my room where I shove my mother's stuff into the box under my bed.

I never called her *Mother* before she died.

Dad sends me out for some cigarettes after dinner, and as I walk past the church opposite Degrazis' neighborhood grocery store there's a sign outside: *Life's short, God's infinite.*

I spit into the gutter. Then I cross the road to buy Dad his cigarettes.

My father sleeps next to a gap. My mother lies in the earth. Adam's dreaming of the big deal. Me, I may never sleep again until I do what must be done.

RANDOM LIGHT

DAWN'S LEAKING INTO MY ROOM when I wake up. There's a mynah bird tapping on the window and a faint smell of smoke. My ass is itchy. I get this far before I submit to the sensation of being cored and see my mother being lowered into the ground. In a box.

Day seven.

Better than yesterday. At least now I know what I have to do.

In this world there are answers for all kinds of shit. All you need is the right question.

I pull out my notebook, most of its pages still blank, and write:

1. Why did she die?

Because she got slammed by a car going too fast, weighing too much, filled with the velocity of somebody not giving a damn about other people's lives.

I saw an old guy get hit by a Volvo once, down by the shops. Saturday afternoon, about to sink my teeth into a spearmint chocolate chip ice cream cone, and this guy's flying, doing a slow-motion twirl. The weirdest thing was his shoe. It had a life of its own, like a leather bird riding the thermals in an upward spin, his foot reaching toward it, never quite making it, all so slow and graceful and not quite Saturday afternoon, and then the thud of him landing behind the car. The stillness in the wake of it, before I dropped my ice cream and people remembered that they were meant to help. And then *it* landed. The old guy's shoe. Dropped between a woman carrying a baby and a guy in a suit, and I remember thinking, *Lucky no one got hurt.*

Don't know what happened to the old guy in the end. I took off telling myself I was too young to be of help—at twelve I knew nothing about death. But what does anyone know? Unless you're dead, but hey, that's the biggest joke of all. Unless you believe those people who say they died, entered the tunnel, saw the bright light, and came back. Like holding your breath underwater till your lungs become liquid, your arms all limp, and you think, it's up to me now, I can choose. But you can't, your body fights you and says, *Don't think I'm going to let you go.*

It's just oxygen, of course, your lungs screaming out for it. Scream hard enough and you see white light.

Did Mom?

Maybe I have the wrong question:

2. Is it terrifying, the moment of death?

We're not having roast tonight, or pizza. We've been invited to someone's place, for sympathy food. Adam's been out all day catching up with people; on the way back he visited Mom's grave. He's in the kitchen, his face grappling for control, when I come in. "Weird, when you think about it. She'll spend more time in that one place than anywhere else."

"Now look who's getting all deep," I say to smooth the unease of his confession, but all he does is curl his lip, and say, "Prick."

Dad saunters in as Adam goes out.

Dad in one of his talkative moods. "Will."

"Dad."

It's genetic.

He's wearing the green sweater Mom gave him last Christmas. He doesn't like it much—being so tall, he says it makes him look like a tree. We're all tall, a skyscraper family. At least in that sweater he looks as if he's got someone taking care of him. Wonder how long that'll last. "So, whose house are we going to?" I ask.

"Ray's."

"Who's Ray?"

"He was at the wake," says Dad, heading into the hall.

I follow. "Don't remember him."

"He was with his wife and daughter." Dad flattens his hair in the mirror. Mom always did that for him. "I told you about him. He used to go out with your mom."

"We're having dinner with Mom's ex?"

They say loss does strange things.

"Well, sort of. He was also a friend of mine."

"Why don't I know them?"

"It was a long time ago, before you were born."

Adam comes in wearing an ironed shirt. He checks out my old jeans and a T-shirt Mom bought me. At least Adam dresses himself. "I'm meeting some friends for dinner."

"What about Ray's?" Dad asks.

"I'm not coming. I don't even know them." Adam rakes his fingers through his hair in front of the hall mirror. He looks at his watch then back at Dad. "Tom Wallace is picking me up in about ten minutes. You remember Tom."

"Yes, I think so. You drive, Will, you need the practice. Not long till you go for your license now."

Dad drops the keys into my hands and heads out the front door.

"Nice work," I say, nudging past Adam.

"What?" He raises his eyebrows and goes back to realigning his hair, his reflection blocking mine, except for a slice of my head. He is my brother but he is closed to me.

If I had my notebook I'd write:

3. Why do some get to live, and others die?

Ray's house is yellow. Below the knocker, there's a sticker, *We acknowledge the Wurrundjeri people as the traditional owners of this land.* A political front door. They can't be friends of Dad's. It opens.

"Ray, how are you?"

"Good, thanks, Michael. Come in. And you must be Will," says Ray, shaking my hand. He's much thinner than Dad. His gray hair is pulled back into a ponytail and he's wearing a black shirt. I manage a smile as he takes us through to the living room. The walls are crowded with paintings and framed posters, the coffee table full of homemade dips and stuff. The whole house has a congested feel.

"So, Will. Are you still studying?"

"Yeah. I'm in Year 12."

His ponytail brushing his shoulders, Ray gives Dad a knowing look. "So you've got exams coming up soon?"

"Mmmm," I nod, recognizing one of the posters—it's of the South American guy from that movie, the one where he becomes a revolutionary after crossing the continent on a motorcycle.

"Taryn!" calls out Ray, and she runs in. I can't believe it; it's the girl from the dream. The one who wore white to the wake. "You remember Michael, and this is Will."

"Hi," she says, her tooth resting on her lip.

"Hi." The taste of chocolate in my mouth. I focus on that poster. Che, that's who he is, Che Guevara, the certainty of his name helping to keep the blood out of my cheeks. But Taryn's not helping. She's sitting next to Ray, inspecting us, the way we move, letting her eyes run all over us, and mostly over me.

"Taryn's a year behind you at school, Will," says Ray, spilling dip on his chin. "So, Michael, you're already back at work?"

"Couldn't see any point in taking extra time off."

Taryn leans over, her hair so long it sweeps my knee. "Will, there's something I want to show you."

She stands, her skirt taking a moment to fall down her leg, and I follow her, because right now she's my white rabbit, except her hair's the color of the cat Mom used to have. Marmalade. It was her cat, she always said, because she never had a girl. Figure the logic. I want to ask Taryn where we're going, except it doesn't matter; there's something about her feet, the way they rise up to me naked and pale, a little pink around the edges.

"Thought they might need some time alone," she says.

We're in the kitchen, and she's filling glasses with water, her finger touching mine as she hands one to me. This time my cheeks refuse to oblige. I go for cover at the table that squats in the middle of the room. "Where's your mom?" I ask.

"She's late but she should be here soon."

"Are you an only child?"

"No. I have two sisters, but one's in India, and the other one is out. Couldn't do the mourning thing with strangers."

I want to ask her if she can but the words dissolve as she smiles and hooks her hair behind her ears. Taryn. She has green eyes, freckles on her cheeks, a small scar above her lip—beautiful, that's all there is to think about her. The sinkhole in my stomach fills a little. I close my mouth.

"I can't imagine . . ." She frowns.

"What?"

"Do you want to break things?"

I want to break the whole world open, dig around in its entrails till I find some answers, but I don't think that's what she means. Taryn goes over to the bench, draws a psycho-sized knife out of a block, holds it up in front of her before passing it, hilt first, to me. It's heavy in my hand but it feels like someone else is holding it.

"Cut into the table," she says, "like this." She puts her hands, warm beyond reason, around mine and drags them across the surface, slicing a groove with the knife. Her breath smells of lime. Letting go, she whispers, "Go on, it's all right."

So I do, I carve into the wood and feel its softness as it gives in to the blade, hardly any resistance at all. If I slip, it'll cut straight through me it's so sharp; it won't worry about flesh and bone, just keep going till it's made its way to the other side. There's something gratifying in the way the wood submits.

"I did that when my boyfriend dumped me last year. It felt great."

I can't imagine anyone leaving her. She traces her finger over a long groove next to mine.

"Was your mom beautiful? Dad said she was."

"I . . ." Someone else is in the reflection of the knife.

"Mom, finally." Taryn grips her mother's shoulder. They turn toward me, their mouths so alike, both small.

"Sorry, traffic was a nightmare. I'm Sandra."

As I put down the knife she holds out her hand. It's cold. Smooth.

"I'm Will."

"Will, I was sorry to hear about your mother. I knew Anna well when we were younger. Wish we'd got back in contact earlier, but you know how it is."

My eye is drawn to the freshly carved groove. It's about the length of my forearm, the raw wood lighter than the varnished surface, barely visible, the color of flesh. They're both watching me, these women, and suddenly all their sincerity feels like grabbing. "I should be getting back."

Sandra nods. "Of course. I'll be there in a minute."

She goes over to the sink, her jacket pulling across her shoulders, her hair rolled up in a ball at the base of her neck.

Taryn follows me, touches my arm, whispers, "You know, once you've carved into our table, you're one of us."

I look at her hand and for a moment it all feels creepy, this family with their table witness to their lives. But she's close, so close I can smell her, her scent wrapping itself around me, filtering its way in.

4. Is it possible for others to taste your pain?

After dinner, while Dad's in the bathroom, Ray says, "I know your dad's a bit on the quiet side, so if you need someone to talk to."

I look at this man I've only just met, his nose that's lost its way, one of his front teeth dead.

"Will, your mom and I, a long time ago . . ." He checks the door through which Sandra left. "A long time ago, we were close."

There's an unwieldy silence; his confession has no place to go.

"You'll come back, won't you, Will?" asks Taryn, and I know I must. There's something about how they hang together, the way they're allowing me in.

"Sure," I say to her.

I want to touch her freckles, one by one. They're like constellations—make me think that if I joined them together, dot to dot, some map to the universe would appear across her face.

5. When one thing ends, does another always begin?

Dad's staring into the absence of traffic as he drives us home. His neck looks older, the skin darker—it's a long time since I really looked at my father, how he holds the steering wheel, pushing it away from him, his obsession with adjusting mirrors as if it will somehow save him from his fate. My father has friends I never knew about and together they have a past, a pool of memories. Jesus, for all I know, tonight I met my mother's one true love.

Dad stops at the lights. People cross the road in front of our car but they don't see us, father and son, side by side. Eight days beyond Anna's death. On my leg is a CD Taryn slid into my hand as I left. I try to read the song titles in the unpredictable light, to work out which one will give me an answer.

6. How many questions does it take?

THE ULTIMATE TRUTH

THE WIND IS WARM and it feels good to be out walking; at home the walls and floors are made of glue. It's not far to the local library but even the birds seem to be doing Saturday morning slowly.

As the doors whoosh open, I remember the last time I was here, with Mom, her walking ahead of me, her red hair, just dyed, clashing with her coat, a stack of books in her arms. I almost decide to go home, but picture Dad still ruminating over his cornflakes and decide to stay—besides, last time I checked there were no answers scrawled across my bedroom wall.

There's a computer free in the center of the library and another one taken hostage by a couple of kids perfecting their vocabulary on sex. I hear them talking about looking up *orgasm* as I type *death* in the subject box and hit *enter*. There are 457 listings—on the first page, some graphic novels and abstractly linked titles, before I find the number that I need: 155.

I look around and remember where things are. Down by the long windows that drop into nowhere, I work my way along to 155, the books on grief, some devoted to dying, some written for kids. I pick one out because of its yellow cover, its plastic spine warm from the sun. The book lists the stages of mourning, each phase spelled out in detail with headings, all so precise, the anatomy of grief, and I have an urge to tear it into tiny, precise pieces, but a lifetime of respect for books works against my desire for revenge. I return it to the shelf, lean against the cookery books opposite, and wonder what to do next. If only there was one titled *A Thousand Recipes for Dealing with Your Own Mortality*, but chocolate seems to be the main theme here.

The sun through the windows warms my feet through my shoes. Above the books on grief are some on philosophy—by names like Plato, Bertrand Russell, Marcus Aurelius, the same book as Mom's. Next to it, there's one called *On the Shortness of Life*. I pull it out and flick through it till I find this: *It is better to conquer our grief than deceive it . . . But the grief that has been conquered by reason is calmed forever.*

This is better—I prefer the sound of *conquering* to squeezing the havoc in my head into a neat little box. I sit on the carpet and pull out my notebook, with its spiral binding and black cover, about the same size as most of these philosophy books. On the first page, *Will Ellis* is written in big letters like a title.

I turn to where I wrote my questions and copy the sentences opposite them, the ones about grief, and with each word I feel a part of me loosen, smoothing the jaggedness of my thoughts. The cover of *On the Shortness of Life* is white, the lettering all embossed, good to run your finger over, and according to the blurb on the back it's by a philosopher called Seneca. He's talking to a friend of his, Paulinus, explaining to him about life: *It is not that we have a short time to live, but that we waste a lot of it.*

Waste. This afternoon I was thinking of having another listen to that CD Taryn gave me, to get past the music and into the words. Maybe go around and see Seb. Is that *waste*? And how do you deceive grief?

I riffle through the book to see what else Seneca has to say—the problem is he keeps getting off the track, talking about gladiatorial contests and someone called Scipio. An old guy reading a newspaper over by the window tilts forward and farts, turns the page, doesn't even flinch. Man, the bravado of the old. Here it is: you deceive grief by distracting yourself, says Seneca, by turning your back on the big questions. A man after my own heart. What you need instead is philosophy and reason.

Philosophy and reason.

And I know as I read this that he's talking about more than one book from your local library, even if it is his. I'm going to need shelves of them, a whole world of ideas to arm myself against ignorance, the kind that lets in pain. That's if you believe a guy who's been dead for two thousand years. *For only philosophy . . . can divert from its anguish a heart whose grief springs from love.*

Behind me a woman calls out to her daughter who's tipping books off the shelves, watching them flap like paper birds. She must be about two, the kid, and she's ecstatic, as if she's finally discovered why everyone's so enchanted by books. Her fingers are fat and unruly and there's chocolate bracketing the corners of her mouth. She hauls out a hardcover book, *Mastering Philosophy*, and holds it up to me, grinning as she drops it on my leg with a thud. It falls open and halfway down the page it says: *The study of ultimate reality.*

"Riana." The woman grabs hold of the kid's shoulders, and spins her around.

"It's okay, I'll pick them up," I say, rubbing my knee.

"Thanks." The woman whips her daughter up into her arms

and the kid kisses her on the nose, cheeks, eyes and makes her mother laugh. Little but smart. I guess I was smart like that once, when things were simple and life was all about chocolate and keeping out of trouble.

Maybe it still is.

Dad's working in his study, Adam's out for lunch, so I grab a Mars bar and leave a note: *Back for dinner, Will.*

At the train station, there's a guy harvesting dropped tickets, hoping to find one he can use. Hate that—he looks about my dad's age; he should have the cash. He's still searching as the train pulls in, and out.

There are a couple of kids I know with skateboards, and we nod, but I don't want to talk. Instead I look out the window of the train and lose myself in the rattling past of things—people's backyards, their washing, some woman's red undies flailing in the wind. I half imagine how that woman might look as I close my eyes, think of Taryn, and that knife, a red Honda crashing into Mom. I open my eyes to a sign nailed up on somebody's tree: *Jesus is coming soon. Prepare for His return.*

At the next station, a woman in a bright orange sweater gets on carrying a silver bag in the shape of an egg. She shuffles over to the window across from me, so I have to fold my knees in. On her foot, a tattoo. It says *serendipity,* which I remember from that film where they fall for each other but leave meeting again to chance.

When I stare at her foot, the woman smiles at me. "Do you believe in fate?" she asks, and for a minute I think she's coming on to me, but what are the chances of that?

"Fate?"

"Yeah, you know, if things are meant to happen, they will."

"Don't know," I say, looking out the window.

"It's all about watching out for the signs." She pulls her bag in closer to her stomach. I can see her reflection in the glass; her nose is pierced and the stud keeps catching the light.

"Signs?"

"Haven't seen any today," she says, turning to look at a tall woman who's shouting down at the other end of the car, shouting at herself. "What about you?"

They keep slapping me in the face, I think, staring at fences, though I'm not sure what you're meant to do with random pages, a poster about Jesus, and a foot about fate. Where's the equation? Maybe you need to throw something in sideways, see what comes out. "My mother died. Nine days ago."

Her hand goes to her mouth, "Oh, really."

"Yeah, really. Where's the serendipity in that?" I'm being an asshole, I know, but maybe I can jolt her into some truth.

"I . . . I'm not sure." She's getting up, pulling that bag in closer, its silver strap dangling over her wrist. "Um, this is my stop. Wow, I'm sorry."

She stoops toward me for a second, and then she goes, steps out onto the platform and keeps walking without looking back, till that tattoo of hers blurs into a smudge. A black cat sitting on a wall watches the train pull out.

Flinders Street Station is manic, even considering it's the center of Melbourne. People dodge each other as they go where they need to be, but I can't get into the flow. I bang into three people, all wearing suits, all women. "Sorry," I say, "Sorry," and one more time. "Sorry! For Christ's sake!"

My ticket gets stuck in the machine on the way through and some Indian guy in an orange vest has to help me out. I push past the guy selling flowers, buckets of nature lined up against the gray, and then out into the light. People pour down the steps but I let them flood around me—I don't even know where the State Library is, so there's no rush. Saturday afternoon and I'm on my second library. Loss does strange things.

It's hot, hot on my face, on my chest, and the warmth feels good; it's evaporating something that doesn't belong. I find a spot on the steps out of the traffic but still in the sun. Below me, there are some emos huddled in as much shade as they can manage, a flock of them all in black like suicidal crows. One of them's standing up and he's thin and pale and so vampirish I almost laugh out loud; he's even wearing a black cape. Wonder if he sleeps in a coffin, bites chicks on the neck. He certainly has them enthralled, with their fishnet stockings and black lipstick smiles. He's their god, no doubt about it as they watch his every move, the flop of his hair over his left eye, his long fingers that twist and dive as he speaks. He breathes confidence like fresh air. He's almost wonderful—I want to hear what he's saying, but don't want to catch his eye.

And then he flinches. It's instantaneous, but there's a glitch in his calm, as if he suddenly remembered who he is and, for a split second, let the world in. He leans back into himself, flicks his hair out of his eyes, revealing his T-shirt underneath the cape. And on it is written: *God is dead.*

A man going past in a dark suit scoffs, "What would a punk know about Nietzsche?"

The sun steals behind a cloud. One of the emo girls laughs.

* * *

I enter the stream of bodies, make for the pub across the road and exit the heat. As I'm tall for my age, people think I'm older, so I shouldn't have any trouble getting served. I've never tried before but I don't feel like going to the library yet; I feel like parking myself beside a bunch of guys and drinking beer—making some sense of the signs, if that's what they are.

Downstairs it's smoky and there are mostly men, not men in suits, but casual Saturday afternoon gear. The guy behind the bar is shorter than me, but he's got arms like trunks. "A beer, please."

"Got any ID?"

"Not on me," I say, touching my pockets, half believing I can conjure one up.

"No ID, no beer. Sorry."

"No worries," I say, hoping charm will get me through, except I'm a bit short on it today. The guy pulls out a rack of clean glasses, wipes the few that aren't dry, lines them up inverted on a green mat. He moves fast, his fingers hefty, but nothing breaks. Once he's finished, he turns back to me and grins. "You still here?"

I spin a coaster on the bar, and each time it lands the same way up. Half the world must walk through this bar, talk to this guy, tell him stuff, so I figure I'll try my luck. "Do you know who Nietzsche is?"

"Do I look like I might?"

"Maybe."

He looks at me out of the corner of his eye as he checks a glass and serves a beer to a guy wearing a beret. "You should go," he says.

"I'm waiting for a friend."

"Look, kid, maybe you'd be better off waiting outside."

"I'm eighteen, you know."

"Like hell you are."

I think of the Jesus sign impaled on a tree, the vampire guy and the woman with her stupid tattoo, all so bloody random. "Why don't you just fuck off."

"Go now before I get you thrown out."

He's got his chin thrust at me. I can tell he's dying to hit me, and I want to punch him back, smack him straight in his red moon face. "If you lay a hand on me I'll sue you," I grin.

"You little prick." His nostrils flare. Those fists could pulverize me, no question, but I need to see how far he'll go, how much he can hate somebody he doesn't even know. If I'm worth his job.

"Pussy." Something inside me cringes. *This isn't you, Will*, it says, but there's no way in hell that I can know that, if I never put myself to the test. The guy's swallowing back his fury, his veins bulging trails across his temple. The clingy smell of old beer.

"Lyle, what's the story?" A young guy comes over, his eyes roving between the barman and me. He's not happy. "I think you'd better go, kid. Take your shit somewhere else."

So I do. I pick up my backpack, and me and my shit, we head for the door, away from barmen who know nothing about Nietzsche, who won't serve me beer. And I take with me one thought. If God is dead, who killed him?

I might find the answer at the library, but I'm not in the mood for books anymore. Not much in the mood for anything. Right now, I reckon I've got as much chance of finding what I'm looking for on a T-shirt. Or somebody's foot.

Back on the steps outside the station, while the emos squint in the sun, I pull out my notebook and write:

7. What is my life worth?

On the way home on the train there are no signs, or if there are I decide not to look. Instead I study my hands because I know them and they've never revealed anything to me before. Except there's a cut on my left thumb and I stare at it, trying to remember when I did it, whether it was before or after Mom died.

After.

I sliced it with the pizza cutter—too busy theorizing with Adam about what's best: classic crust or pan-fried. Arguing over pizza, now that's certainly a waste of life. So is picking fights, especially with bulldog barmen. He could've killed me. Maybe right now that's the kind of response I need to feel alive.

When I get home, after I've washed the city off me, I go online and do a little searching. Seneca was a Roman philosopher who died a slow and painful death at the whim of Emperor Nero. Nietzsche was a German philosopher who went mad. Not the best advertisements for philosophy, but so far it's the only thing I've got.

Over dinner I decide to try them. "If God's dead, who killed him?"

"Christ!" says Adam.

"Unlikely," I say, biting into a chip.

Dad, through a mouthful of fish: "Who says God is dead?"

FREE FALL

MEMORY.

My first of my mother. I'm in my crib, half-awake, tangled in a sheet, and I can't find my way out. Everything is yellow. Her voice through the folds, *You're okay, Will*, her cool hands reaching in, easing me free. Her face altered by fear, her squeeze more suffocating than the sheet. But in her grasp, I relax, and no longer struggle to breathe.

Monday. Day 11. Alone again.

Dad's at work and Adam's out somewhere trying to wangle himself a high-paying job—he's decided to stay, ditch his career in Malaysia. So far he hasn't said why. I should be at school but Dad's letting me take time off. I seem to be the only one.

In my hand is my mother's camera. The back, where you open it to put the film, is like elephant skin. It's much heavier than Adam's digital that he bought on his way home. I run my finger over its forms, its division into rough and smooth, black and silver, plastic and glass. On the side of the viewfinder, there's a gold sticker with the word *passed* barely visible, it's been handled so often. And there's the dent and its suggestion of guilt. I wipe dust off the glass of the frame counter, the white line pointing to the number *28*. Twenty-eight pictures contained in there still undeveloped.

The last ones my mother took.

I go past Degrazis' and the church. The sign's still there. The parking lot outside the supermarket is hectic, shiny cars lined up in the heat. It's too warm for September, the seasons in this city as impulsive as ever, not even a cloud to remind us it's spring.

"It will take a day to get the photos developed." That's what the woman in the camera shop says as she picks off chunks of pink nail polish. One lands on my mother's film but I leave it with her anyway.

Out in the open again under a tree, I sit on a bench next to an old lady. The bags under her eyes are resting on her cheeks. She doesn't smile—maybe I've got too big. I take Mom's camera out of my backpack and load it with a new roll of film I found on the top shelf in our fridge where Mom keeps them. Kept them. The old woman's wearing a pale green cardigan even in this heat—she must be too old for weather—and her body is all curled in on itself. My mother would have taken a photograph of her if she could. Up close. That's the way she liked to look at people, at their most intimate. I don't think I could do that.

There's a fluffy white dog attached to a chair outside the café opposite, but no owner in sight. It's drinking out of a stainless steel bowl and there's a nicely distorted reflection but I can't think of a good reason to take a picture of a dog, of anything. Maybe it's too hot. I look over at the cars. Cars are not my thing, though there's an old green one the color of spearmint ice cream and it even has those tires with a white rim, a metallic beauty to it, headlights like eyes.

I step out into the sun, a season ahead of itself, and lift Mom's camera to my face; the car looks reduced through the lens. I bring the image into focus, the glint of the chrome, the fish-eyed reflection of the car next to it, the crisscross patterns of the lights.

The fender.

I hear the camera shutter clunk, the sound of a screeching brake, and feel the body of the camera shift. The fender is perfectly curved and it returns the light. Fender. The instrument of my mother's death.

Tuesday, I call the camera shop to see if my photos are ready—I ended up finishing the whole new roll. I pick them up, mine and Mom's, her last twenty-eight pictures. Every one intact.

Day 13.

We get another invite from Taryn's family—Adam's not coming; he's going out with friends again. I drive. On the way over Dad says, "When I met your mom she had long hair."

"I know, I've seen the photo," I say, checking his face for meaning, but his eyes are focused beyond the road. It's a color photo and the two of them are sitting on a log at a beach, their arms loose around each other's waists. All the other photos in the album are in black-and-white—Mom preferred to use black-and-white film—most are of Dad, or people I don't know. As always, close up.

"It suited her," he says. "She should've kept it long." His hand absently skirts the edge of my seat. "There are a lot of things we should've done."

* * *

We eat kangaroo steaks cooked on the barbecue, medium rare—when I cut into mine, the blood pools on my plate. Dad turns his attention from Ray and Sandra to me; he's looking for something. "This is the first time we've eaten kangaroo, isn't it, Will?"

"Yes, Dad, it is."

We all watch as he nudges a potato across his plate, but he's got nothing more to say. Ray starts up their conversation again as Taryn licks her fingers, her hair dipping in her food. We're at the groove end of the table. "So, did you like that CD?" she asks.

"It's not the kind of thing I usually listen to but it was all right."

"Samara got me into Jeff Buckley."

"Is she one of your sisters?"

"Yeah. She's in India but she's coming home soon. Won't stay long though, she never does."

"Wouldn't mind taking off myself."

"Where would you go?"

"Anywhere," I say, putting down my fork.

"You're not hungry, are you?" whispers Taryn, running her finger along the groove I carved. It's already beginning to darken from exposure to the air.

"Not really."

Dad looks up from his plate as Taryn stands. "Mom, I'm going to show Will the mandala."

"Sure. I'll call you for dessert," says Sandra, catching Taryn's hand as we go past. Eyes on me, Sandra goes to speak, but I keep moving. Their kitchen smells of spice, ours smells of lemons.

The backyard has paths meandering through frames with plants growing up them, past wooden seats, a pond with a concrete Buddha watching over it. The sun is low in the sky, tracing everything in orange, the scent of some flowers sickly sweet as we go past. "Night jasmine," says Taryn, as she disappears behind a tree.

I follow her into an opening where she's pointing at her feet.

"We made it last time Samara was here."

It is a large circle, circles within circles, like a zodiac. I crouch down and touch it.

"It's mostly tiles, some we painted, some we fired ourselves," she says proudly. "We've got a kiln near the shed."

Her face is golden in the sinking light. She's all gold, even her dress that stops above her knees. She shivers and I think I'd lend her my jacket if I had one—I want to give her something but I have nothing to give.

"You can sit on it if you want. Mandalas are meant to be ephemeral."

"Ephemeral?"

"In Tibet, monks make them out of colored sand and as soon as it's finished they destroy it with the sweep of a hand." Taryn passes her arm parallel to the mandala and flicks her wrist dramatically as I run my fingers over the ridges of a tile glazed with a star. She leans in. "It's supposed to symbolize the impermanence of life."

The impermanence of life? She looks beautiful, her face so willing in the orange light, but right now this is not what I need. What I need is some forensic show on TV, Dad on the couch half reading the newspaper, and Mom . . .

"Is this meant to be some kind of lesson?"

"Sorry."

She shivers again, takes hold of my hand and kisses it on the palm. We don't move. Her green eyes. The warm tiles still holding the heat of the sun. The light sitting on her top lip like a gold bow.

Slowly she slides my hand around her neck, over her shoulder, and presses her forehead into mine, rolling it back and forth like my mom's cat used to until you could feel the bones of its skull beneath the fur.

She's close, so close the first tears wet both her cheeks and mine, and for a moment I'm not sure whose they are, but as one makes its way into my mouth I recognize the taste of it. Or do hers have that same saltiness as mine?

I didn't cry when I heard the news. Seb's mom came into his room, and there was Dad, tall behind her, both of them hushed, and I remember thinking *This is what pale looks like,* and then, *Who died?*

"It's your mother," said Dad as he led me to the car. He drove us to the hospital, our silence defying her death, me wondering all the time why he couldn't have left me that little bit longer in my other world—the one where I had a mother. Where things didn't weigh so much and feel so light.

I wipe my eyes with the back of my sleeve and lean in till her face is made up of pieces I'm so close, her freckles blurred, and I kiss her, like I've never kissed anybody, the divide fading between her body and mine.

"Taryn! Will! Dessert!" Sandra's voice travels across the garden in the night. We pull back, breathing like we've been wrestling.

"Are you okay?" I whisper.

"Sure," says Taryn, dragging me up, the pattern of a half-moon pressed into her calf. The bones of her fingers thread through mine as she leads me along the path.

"They're good people," says Dad, sticking the key in the ignition. "Do you want to drive?"

"No, you can," I say, leaning into the headrest. I spot a star between the branches of a tree, more lucid than all the others in the night sky.

8. *Is there such a thing as fate?*

When we get home, Dad sprawls in front of the TV in the living room and I think about joining him but he flicks to the news. Adam's still out. I go into the study, turn on the computer, and go to Taryn's page on Facebook. She's online. I send her a message.

I have a question for you.
Will

Sure,
T

If you were on the 102nd floor of the south tower of the World Trade Center when the roof was caving in, would you have jumped?

OK, that kind of question. Would I jump? I'd like to think I would. I've always wanted to fly. Hasn't everyone? To choose the way I die.

But imagine standing at the window, the glass all gone, the roar of the fire and the wind and the sirens below you, knowing you've got no chance of getting out alive, thinking, maybe, if I jump, something, some miracle might suck me through a window on a floor below. That my courage, my belief will save me. Single me out.

I'm not sure I believe in miracles, Will. At least they got to free-fall off a tower in Manhattan. There's a kind of poetry to that.

Will?

Poetry in death?

The light from the screen defines us against the dark. Poetry in death: I go into my room and from the box under my bed I pull out the photos I took the other day. When I've found the one I'm looking for, I return to the study, lay it facedown on the scanner, the image uploading in layers like a memory. I paste it into my album and send her the link.

Dream.

Dust. The ground moves beneath my feet. They are bare and now they no longer touch the earth. My body tips, my arms outstretched, the sun warm on my back. I rise higher, each movement of shoulder or wrist alters my direction. The wind buoys me and I soar, riding the thermals, beyond, so high.

Too high.

I dip my head, go into a dive. The ground is white and blurred below me but as I draw closer I see its details. The dust has turned to stone and ruptured into jagged rocks.

I plummet.

When I wake, the dream's still hanging over me and there's an image I can't quite let go of—a single white feather drifting to the ground. The house is subdued. It's only 8:05, too early for Dad and Adam to be gone. I try to remember what day it is; Thursday, I think. On the way home last night, Dad tried to talk about my exams coming up, about returning to things, but when I maintained my silence his focus went back to the road.

I haul myself up and go into the study to see if Taryn has replied. Fish are swimming across the screen.

OK, Will, it's my turn. Question. What is happiness?

T ♥

No comment about the photo. Happiness? I go onto one of those quote Web sites I've been checking out lately, type in *happiness*, and scroll through till I find one I like.

The mind is its own place, and in itself
Can make a heaven of hell, a hell of heaven.

John Milton

Will XX

Good morning, Will. You got that off one of those quotation sites, didn't you? Cheat. So, what do you think about this?

There is only one happiness in life, to love and be loved.

George Sand

T ♥

OK. But isn't it dangerous loving someone when you know they're going to die?

Of course, but what choice have we got?

At the park later that morning, there's a flock of white cockatoos strutting around a pile of feed someone's left. As I approach, lens first, some of the birds sidle away, others stay, intent on the food. They tip their yellow crests as I get closer, one of them thrusting his gray beak at me with a screech. I crouch, but as my knee cracks, a cloud of them takes off in a rush of wind and I catch the spread of a wing through the lens. It looks like the wings of angels you see in paintings, though these noisy birds are about the furthest thing from angelic. But then I remember something Mom told me when I was little. She said for the Aborigines the cockatoo was seen as a messenger.

SETTING SAIL

IN THE BOX UNDER MY BED, I also keep the last photos my mother ever took. There are some of us on a picnic in the mountains before Adam went away last time, a close-up of Dad, his back against a peeling gum tree. He looks happy though I remember him getting pissed off soon after because he'd forgotten his binoculars and wanted to see the view. Mom handed him her camera and told him to look through the zoom lens instead. And there's a picture of me, my hair still long, before I cut it off, the dimple in my chin like Mom's. I'm not looking at the camera. It's as if I've seen a ghost.

The State Library has the right architecture for wisdom. Columns. A statue of Joan of Arc. I thought about calling Taryn and asking her if she wanted to come, but she's probably got better things to do on a Saturday. Most people do.

"It's my first time here," I say to the woman at the information desk. She smiles, gives me a map, and marks a cross where the philosophy books are.

"This is a reference library," she says, "so you can't borrow anything. Most of the first editions are in storage." And I think, what would it be like to shake the dust off a few of those, smell the original ideas?

I go up the stone staircase into a gallery of paintings, through the doors to the reading room. It's massive. People are sitting at tables, lost in books and laptops, plugged in at booths, as I follow my map to 190, where the philosophers live. There are two whole rows of books, some on Western philosophers, most I've never heard of, others on Confucianism, Chinese ethics, shamanism, whatever that is, and all the big religions. Books with titles like *Does God Exist?*, *The Troubadour of Knowledge*, *Experiments Against Reality*, *The Truth About Everything*, *The Guide of the Perplexed*.

There are even books about mourning, one called *The Gift of Death*. Maybe I'll look at that one later. Nobody else is in this row so I sit on the floor, prop my back against the books. I didn't sleep well last night, kept waking up halfway through dreams I couldn't remember, like snatching at fog. All I have with me is my notebook and a pen; I had to leave my bag in the locker with Mom's camera in it. Hope it's all right.

I turn toward the shelf, see a title I like, *The Laughter Is on My Side*—comedy in the philosophy section; I could do with a bit of a laugh. It's about a guy called Søren Kierkegaard. Good name, Søren. I flick through to a chapter called "The Midnight Hour" and find a sentence of his—he was twenty-two when he wrote it, according to the dates; only five years older than me. *The thing is to find a truth which is true for me, to find the idea for which I can live and die.*

I shift my back, books digging into my spine. An idea for which I could live and die. But how to track it down among all these books, so many thinkers with different views of the world. And this is only one row among millions—Jesus, I might as well go home. Though, it could feel good to pile knowledge up against that ignorance Seneca talked about, the kind that lets in pain. But does knowledge equal happiness? I turn to Søren again, go through his words till I find this bit; it's like he's reading my mind. *It is only after a man has thus understood himself inwardly, and has thus seen his way, that life acquires peace and significance.*

I guess he's not talking about world peace, more the settling of the fight within myself. Like with Dad. There are times I want to go up to him and say, *It fucking hurts,* grab hold of him, squeeze him hard. But there are other times I never want to see him again because the pain on his face mirrors my own.

Somebody's phone goes off. It belongs to a girl huddled over a laptop at the end of the row. She looks Chinese. Beside her is a stack of texts, philosophy maybe, or economics for all I know. So many books, so many lives.

I feel like I've been in the bath too long. I need air. The front lawn outside the library would be good right now, thick squares of green lying under the sun. I've got a cheese sandwich in my bag in the cloakroom, and a banana—hope it's not squashed, especially as Mom's camera's in there—but before I go I need to find Nietzsche. I still don't know if he's the one who killed God.

His books are on the opposite side of the row. There are loads about his ideas, and some Nietzsche wrote himself, one with a great title, *Thus Spake Zarathustra, A Book for All and None*. The girl on the phone is whispering loudly in Mandarin, sounds like swearing, and people are starting to eye each other. This is a place of silence; her anger isn't allowed. Someone goes *shhh* and it sounds rebellious against the hush.

I let my head drop back against the books and breathe in their musty smell. They're hard, the covers, no comfort here, but if I keep looking, maybe I'll find the one.

Nietzsche says some harsh things about women. Guess it was the time in which he lived, or maybe if he'd got laid more often it would have changed his whole view on life. One thing's for sure—he was a guy who lived and died for an idea.

Out on the lawn I lie back, hands behind my head, face in the sun. There's the noise of trams and voices and birds all merging together as my body sinks into the grass—I have spent the morning with dead people but they seem incredibly alive. I roll over, open up my notebook, and read through a quote I copied down from Nietzsche:

> *We have left the land and taken to our ship! We have burned our bridges—more, we have burned our land behind us! Now, little ship, take care! The ocean lies all around you; true, it is not always roaring, and sometimes it lies there as if it were silken and golden and a gentle favorable dream. But there will be times when you will know that it is infinite and that there is nothing more terrible than infinity . . .*

I pull Mom's camera out of my pack—it's warm and smells of banana—and hold it up to my eye. Focus. The straight lines of the columns, the shine of statues, a bronze flag in the wind. Joan of Arc. She was still a teenager, wasn't she, when she died defending what she believed? I have to be careful that each photo I take is properly framed. So different from digital. I imagine my mother's eye pressed against the viewfinder—she once looked at the world through this small square of glass, defining what she saw, as I do now.

I swap the camera for my notebook.

9. Am I ready for the open sea?

Memory.

A blue dress. Sand patterns on her legs. Her stripy towel, same as Dad's. Running into the surf with her, being bowled over, finding my feet. Water drips from her arm as she helps me up. She heads out deeper into the ocean, her body rising and falling with the waves. I think she will be swallowed up, become part of the blue, and I want to shout above the crash and the foam. But in the end the sea gives her back.

WAVES

DAD'S ALWAYS BEEN A BIT of a workaholic, but now he's reckless—Sunday morning and he's in the study, hair feral, finishing off some financial report, and I swear it's the fourth day he's worn that shirt. Adam's having brunch in the city, meeting some people he might work with. I got that much before the conversation skidded into jargon and he lost me. I had the urge to grab his shoulders—he's that little bit shorter than me—shake him and yell, *Hey, Mom's dead.* But I didn't. Instead I said, "Enjoy your brunch."

Then there are the lawns—ours, the next-door neighbors', on both sides, and an old lady's three doors down. They're my responsibility, my way of making some cash. I have to do them once a week this time of the year when the weather is yo-yoing, sun, rain, sun, things growing at a pace beyond reason. Oh well, each centimeter of grass means extra cash. And the stuff keeps pushing through no matter what—no matter what winter we have entered, outside it's still spring.

And tomorrow there's school. Apparently two and a half weeks are enough to get over the loss of a parent. *You need to focus on your exams,* that's what Dad said, right after I asked him, *For what do you live and die?*

Taryn,

I'm going back to school tomorrow. Can you meet me after?

Come to my place. Nobody else'll be home.

T ♥

See you there.

Love,

Will

I know what it feels like to suddenly be an alien in your own world. To have everyone walking small steps around you, some investigating, some ignoring your every move. The first lot are seeking signs of familiarity, of life. The second are so scared of what your experience might reveal about themselves, they prefer to keep their eyes shut.

I'm talking about my Math class. First day back since *the death* and word's got around. Even Seb is acting like I'm a new species. At recess he asks me if there's anything he can get me, and from the look on his face I can't tell whether he's talking about a packet of chips or some supernatural conjuring of my mother. I guess Seb's only trying to help but lately Taryn seems the only one from a neighboring planet. Maybe because she didn't know me before tragedy struck.

* * *

After lunch, in Physics class, this girl called Mel I hardly know stopped by my desk as she was handing out work sheets for Mr. Brooks. She whispered, "My father died last year. Nobody understands if they haven't experienced it—it's like having a secret knowledge." Frowning, she handed me the sheet headed *Interactions of Matter and Light.*

Taryn's house is not far from the train line. It seems more yellow in the four o'clock light, the kind of yellow Dad wouldn't even paint our letterbox. As I go to knock, Taryn opens the door, wearing that same dress that stops above the knee. She smiles at my school shirt.

"Come in."

The house is quiet. In the kitchen, as I watch her fill two glasses with water, I realize I've never seen anything as beautiful as the way her long fingers wrap around the glass. She offers me one. "Hungry?"

I nod. The water tastes like water. From the pantry she takes a chocolate cake with a piece already gone and shifts a knife over it. "How hungry?"

"Very."

She cuts me a huge slice and lifts it, balanced on the knife I used to carve the groove, over to a white plate, and hands me a fork. She takes one too and starts digging in, so sure of herself, and for an instant I want to be her.

"So, do you believe in miracles?" she asks, sliding cake into her mouth.

I remember what she said in her message. "Miracles? Not sure what I believe right now."

"I believe in you," she says, staring at me.

God, how she stares. I am halfway between cringing and falling in love. Outside a dog barks. "You hardly know me," I say.

"I feel like I do."

How I want that to be real, for her to have some special access to my truth.

"You're not so scary, Will Ellis."

"Scary?"

"Don't you find other people frightening? Especially when they have some power over you?"

Her long hair prickles my hand as she presses her lips against mine. So this is how she deals with fear. I pull her in between my legs, stomach against stomach, her skin close beneath her dress, her tongue navigating my mouth. We sway back and forth. She kisses me on the eyes, the cheek, links her fingers between mine and pulls away, takes me with her to a part of the house I've never seen.

"This is my room," she says. It's green, the color of grass in countries where it always rains; in the middle of the room is a double bed, the duvet spilling across the floor. "Should've cleaned up," she says, smiling, and takes off her dress, straight over her head. "Is this okay?"

I nod and touch her stomach, drawing my finger across it until it rests in her belly button. She draws me in and, hips locked, we fall onto the bed. She's small and so alive beneath me as we seek out each other's mouths again.

"Take your jeans off," she says, undoing her bra. "Everything. Don't worry, I've got condoms."

I roll over onto my back and take off my jeans and my shirt, kicking my shoes off as I go. I hesitate when I get to my boxers and for a moment I think, *She's too good at this, I'm obviously not the first,* like the moment should be less perfect if we're not both virgins and pure. But this isn't about purity.

We get under the duvet, her skin against my stomach, both of us naked. As she rolls on the condom, I shudder, and I think I should tell her I've never done this before. I don't dare touch her, my hands are so moist, but she traces my fingers along her stomach, her hair tangling in a finger, hers, mine. My tongue slides into her mouth, and with her other hand, she guides me in between her legs. She gasps and I wonder if I've hurt her.

"Taryn?"

"I'm okay," she says, her finger resting on my mouth. She draws my head into her neck as I move in and out of her, my body, my breath, seeking out their rhythm, and I realize I'm having sex. For the first time. Having sex with Taryn, the girl I didn't even dare kiss as I came in the door. I am inside her, but it's like she's inside me, as if we've always been like this, naked and held in this green room. And then I get that feeling, one that I know even if I've only experienced it on my own before. I won't last long. Oh God, if only . . . and then I'm done, failing to stifle a groan that surprises me it's so loud. She must think I'm such a fool, but, man, it feels great.

"You okay?" she asks, her breath dawdling in my ear.

"Yeah, it was . . ."

I have a whole world of things I want to declare to her but I don't know words that can live up to the task. Is it possible for her to taste my pleasure as well as my pain?

"Shall we stay like this forever?" she whispers.

Her weight pushes the air out of my lungs. "If only we could."

EROSOPHY

DREAM.

She's sitting on me, naked. Stomach to stomach. Her ginger-blond hair tumbles down my back. But as I pull her away to look at her eyes, I realize that in place of her face is my own.

I see her in every girl who has long hair and graceful fingers, who wears dresses that stop above the knee. I see her in the jar of marmalade on the kitchen table over breakfast. Even when Adam says, "I can't believe you, Will," I hear her voice in the word *believe.*

"Will?"

"Yes, Dad."

"Adam's asked you twice to pass the orange juice."

Adam leers over the table. "Get a grip."

Dad frowns at Adam. "I'll be working late again. Will you boys be all right for dinner?"

"I'm meeting some people in Brunswick Street, so you're on your own, Will. As if that'll make any difference."

"I could come home early if you prefer?" suggests Dad.

"I'll be fine," I say, dipping my spoon into my cornflakes which have already gone soggy. I push the bowl away. "I've got some work to do myself."

"Good," says Dad. "Those exams aren't far off."

"Yeah, don't go flunking, Will, just because . . ."

Dad turns away. Adam raises an eyebrow at me. Prick. This morning his eyes are more green than hazel and, as much as I hate it, even they remind me of her.

Eros. It's Greek for the part of love that involves a passionate, intense desire. Sounds about right. Nobody's home yet, so there's no chance of anyone coming in while I've got this stuff on the screen. I can imagine what Adam would say.

It's about the Greek philosopher Plato who said we look for the kind of beauty that reminds us of the ideal, or Form as he called it, in the people we love. I take a bite of my jam sandwich—as I am on my own tonight I couldn't be bothered making dinner. Plato said that what we desire in those we love is some level of perfection that we don't see in ourselves. They fill us with the belief that the world could be a better place.

The world certainly seems much improved today. When I woke up this morning I felt a presence, as if I was no longer alone. I also felt a strong desire to piss.

I scroll farther down the page and find this quote I like. It's from Socrates, Plato's teacher. I write it down in my notebook. A smear of jam not unlike a heart is in the corner of the page. *Love is of necessity a philosopher, thirsting for wisdom as for all forms of beauty . . . a something immortal in mortality.*

Did I fall in love with Taryn because of what happened to Mom? Maybe Adam's got a point, I am morbid, although it does make sense, *something immortal in mortality.* Oh, for Christ's sake, Will, shut up! What I want: I want her here with me, right now, naked or otherwise. I want to know what she thinks about me when I'm not with her, to walk my fingers up her spine. To listen to her heart beneath her dress, to hear her laugh so truly it enters my bones.

I need to be the *most* something, anything, she's ever known.

I key in Taryn's number—I didn't put it into the memory of our home phone in case Adam saw it. Anyway, I already know it by heart. I almost hang up when I hear her voice; she sounds altered over the phone.

"It's Will. How are you?"

"I'm fine. Except I can't eat."

"What's wrong? Are you sick?"

"Well, yes, I guess I am." I hear the smile in her voice and get what she means.

"I keep forgetting things," I say. "I forgot to screw the lid back on the marmalade this morning and Dad picked it up and it smashed on the floor."

"I couldn't eat dinner. Mom's worried I'm anorexic, but I think Dad's worked it out."

I want to ask her if she's ever felt like this about anyone before, but I'm not ready for the answer. "Is this normal?"

"Is normal what you want?"

"No. When can I see you?"

"See me? Is that all you want to do?"

"Not all."

The thought of her and I'm all body parts, a mass of urges. Her voice sounds so close, I can hear the static of her breathing.

"So, what are we going to do now?" she sighs.

The front door closes. Shit, must be Adam. "Listen, my brother's just got home and I don't want him to know."

"Sure. Can't wait to see you."

"Me too . . ." I whisper, but she's already gone.

Dad and Adam are in the living room dissecting the late news. Outside the moon's so clear, but my room's jagged with shadows. I collapse on my bed and undo my zipper. As I think of Taryn, the tang of her skin, the way she tore off her dress, I can feel it all the way up my spine, my butt muscles tightening, a twinge in the small of my back, my breath pacing toward the finish, harder, faster, my whole body coiling in on itself as I throw my other hand across the bed to seek her out. But there's nothing there. Only my own muffled voice.

There's this legend from Plato about love. It says that once man had four hands and four feet, and one head with two faces that looked in opposite directions, and a round body. But mankind was strong and challenged the gods. This angered them, and Zeus decided that to weaken mankind he would cut them in half.

> *After the division the two parts of man, each desiring his other half, came together, and throwing their arms about one another, entwined in mutual embraces . . .*
>
> *So ancient is the desire of one another which is implanted in us, reuniting our original nature, seeking to make one of two, and to heal the state of man.*

I go to send Taryn this quote from Plato, but instead I send her one from a Russian playwright called Anton Chekhov. It says: *Perhaps the feelings that we experience when we are in love represent a normal state. Being in love shows a person who he should be.* And I send a photo I took in our garden, of a bush my mother planted last spring.

Beautiful. White jasmine is the Hindu symbol for love and commitment. Did you know that?

♥ Taryn

No, I didn't.

Or maybe I did.

Memory.

I am fifteen and at the movie theater with my mother. Dad didn't come—he doesn't like movies, they give him a headache. Mom sees me looking at a blond girl. The lights go dim. She leans over with her box of M&M's, pours some into my hand, and whispers, "She's cute." I blush, but I don't think she can see that in the dark. "I remember," she says, "the first time I was really in love. It was like waking up." We both eat M&M's till the box is empty. When we leave the theater, the girl has already gone.

KNOW THYSELF

"So, Will. What do you want to do with your life?"

Adam's stabbing at his peas. Since Dad's defaulted even on his minimalist level of parenting, I think Adam feels he should step up. My first instinct: tell him to get lost. When I was five, I was going to be a volcanologist, spend my days dodging pyroclastic flows and collecting igneous rocks, but now my future seems as full of holes as pumice. Before Mom died, there was this loose agreement about me going to university and studying math—Dad liked it because he thought I might end up working in finance like him, but I was thinking more about the theory of it, going beyond to where things blur. Quantum stuff. I remember Mom laughing, saying, "I want to know God's thoughts; the rest are details." She said it was a quote from Einstein, and after that it was all settled—Will's future off the agenda. But now . . .

"Well?"

Adam's moved on to his steak. I could ask him the same question, what he wants to do with his one, outrageously short life, but something about the way he's peeling a piece of sinew away from the meat stops me. Anyway, a month ago, if someone had said I'd be tracking down philosophers and having sex, I would have told them they'd got the wrong guy.

Imagine you're in the middle of the city, sitting on the concrete steps opposite the railway station, where the backpackers and office workers hang out. They're all sunning themselves and eating their lunch, when this guy comes up to you. He's kind of stubby with a fat gut and a squashed nose, and he sits down next to you on the step—let's even imagine that he's wearing a toga. He throws the dust-rimmed end of it over his shoulder, leans closer, and asks, "Is war bad?"

"Of course it is," you say, moving away along the step a bit. (I reckon he'd smell like damp sheep.) "People get killed."

"People get killed crossing the street. Is crossing the street bad?"

"That's different," you say. "That's an accident."

"So war's bad because people kill other people on purpose?" he says, shading his balding head.

"Well, yes."

"Is there ever a case when it's okay to kill somebody on purpose? When it might even serve some good?"

Your sandwich is curling at the edges, so you figure you might as well show him you can give as good as you get. "Sure, when the person has done something really bad. Someone like Hitler, for example. The world would've been better off if someone had put a bullet to his head."

"Anybody?"

"Well, yeah, he was so bloody evil."

"So it's all right to take a gun to someone's head if you believe them to be evil?"

"Sure, as long as that person really is bad. Everybody knew what Hitler was up to. How could anyone have not wanted him dead?"

"Plenty of people believed what Hitler was doing was good."

At this point you're wondering what a guy in a toga would know about World War II.

"But to get back to your argument—so long as many people accept that what someone is doing is bad, it's okay to kill them? Is that not what we ask soldiers to do? To destroy a perceived evil on our behalf?"

"So you believe war is a good thing?"

"I'm not saying that. I'm merely trying to get you to think clearly about your own beliefs. Enjoy your lunch."

By now, you're wondering who the bastard works for—whether he's a market researcher or some pro-war nut—though he's sown a seed of a thought, *Maybe the whole war issue isn't so clear-cut.*

You look around to see where he's got to. He's hassling some Japanese backpacker three steps up and she's starting to blush. Maybe her English isn't that good. Maybe where she comes from it's strange to be harassed by balding men wearing togas while you're eating your lunch. But that's what Socrates did. Hung around public squares in Athens interrogating strangers to help them work out what they believed, and how to know themselves truly. Got him into shitloads of trouble, but I like it—a rebel philosopher.

I don't wear a toga. I pretend to look at the electronic announcements skidding across the wall of a nearby building, while I work out who to ask first. From here I can see the pub where the barman with trunks for arms nearly hit me, and now I'm about to hassle some random person I've never met. It's also Friday and I should be at school, but they are cutting me a lot of slack because of Mom. Things have been weird lately, but sometimes you have to go with it. Socrates must have had some nerve. Not sure why I'm doing this; maybe I've got rebel blood.

There's a girl not much older than me in a short skirt, trying to cross her legs and eat a salad without showing too much. She's wearing a necklace with a red plastic heart. I sit on the step next to her, not so close she'll think I'm trying to pick her up.

"Excuse me?" It's the girl with the red heart, freckles bridging her cheeks.

"Yeah?"

"Are you looking for something?" she asks.

"Sorry?"

"I thought you might be a tourist."

It's now I notice that she's pretty. "Oh, no, I was . . . um, wondering . . ."

"Yes?"

"Well . . . if life ends with death?"

"Oh."

She looks down at her crossed legs and I wonder how many times Socrates got punched or made people cry. She's obviously working out the best way to tell me to get lost. But she says, "My boyfriend died six months ago. Climbing accident. We used to eat lunch on these steps."

Shit. "Look, I'm sorry you don't have to . . ."

"It's okay," she says, her hand fiddling with her necklace inside her shirt.

"Did he give you that red heart?"

"No, my grandma did, when I was a kid. She's dead too."

This is not what I expected. I try to think of something consoling, but the only words I can conjure are *She's safe now*, thanks to my tragic great-aunts.

"You know something weird," she says. "I used to think it was a shame my grandma never got to meet Sam, but now I imagine that they're both together, sort of watching over me."

A woman walks past, and there's something about her that reminds me of Mom. That's been happening a lot. The girl tucks the heart back into her shirt. "You know, I never told anyone that before. What's your name?"

"Will."

"I'm Laura. I should be getting back to work." She starts walking down the steps, but at the bottom she turns back. "So, I guess, I believe life doesn't end with death."

And then she goes, waddling; you can't take big steps in that kind of skirt. Waddling past a clown juggling firesticks, through a horde of Asian tourists, to the tram stop, all the way holding on to her heart.

Across the road, in St. Paul's Cathedral, people are taking photos of the stained glass windows by the entrance: fractured wings, a hand holding a plume. I've got Mom's camera with me but I don't feel like playing tourist. Mom brought me in here once when we were in the city, to listen to the choir. It's the only time, apart from now, I've been in a church.

A woman is kneeling into the back of one of the pews, her head buried in her hands, but I can't tell whether she's sleeping or praying; maybe God will tap her on the shoulder if she nods off. Who knows, if I sit here long enough, with these elevated ceilings and gold mosaics, even I will hear the voice of God.

Outside, a tram bell breaches the hum of traffic. An American tourist at the gift shop asks, *How much is this angel?* and the praying woman gives a sob. Guess she wasn't asleep. Against the side wall, there are three rows of lit candles and I go over and choose one from the brass bowl—Mom was sort of a Catholic, so I guess I'm allowed. I light it from one of the others and place it in the top row. The flame shifts and I can feel the heat of the candles on my face. I lean closer and stick my finger in the wax; it's hot and liquid and clingy, but it doesn't burn my skin. I do it again and watch the molding of the wax on my finger, a thick layer of it like a cast. If I bend it, it cracks, turns opaque, and peels away from my skin. My fingerprints are embossed in the congealing wax.

A lady beside me frowns. I didn't notice her arrive, but I stare at her now as I run my finger over the flame. If I could read her mind I know it would say, *Delinquent.* The remnants of wax begin to melt and my skin starts to burn. It hurts but it's manageable. I can choose to stop if I want. Not yet. I can still stand it, the smell and a feeling beyond pain. Shit. I jerk my finger out of the flame and plunge it into my mouth.

The woman's gone. She left the same way she arrived, almost supernatural. She probably went to find someone to chuck me out. I wouldn't blame her. This is a place of devotion, of paying respects; I don't belong here. Maybe I should cross the road to that pub, the one with the pig-faced barman, and let the bastard finish me off.

Dream.

Our house shrouded in flames. They rise into the dark, annihilating my voice. My family is inside. Every time I get close, the fire repels me. At the window, I see my mother's hand.

* * *

In the morning Dad asks me what I did to my finger. I tell him I burned it trying to save some toast.

Once Adam and Dad have gone out I head down to the station to take the train. To Half Moon Bay. Mom used to take us there when we were kids, trailing buckets to load with treasure from the sea. I wanted to bring Taryn but she's gone for the weekend on some family thing. In my backpack: my mother's camera and her blue dress.

As I stare out the train window at the stream of graffiti on people's back fences, so many different tags, I think about Socrates, and how he never wrote anything down. Plato recorded most of what we know about him.

Imagine if Adam was in charge of writing down my life. He'd probably call it *The Kid Who Thought He Knew Everything*, or *The Mad Bastard*, depending on how generous he was feeling. If Dad wrote it he'd call it . . . actually I have no idea. And, me, I think, I'd call my autobiography *The Book of Questions*. But which one of these versions would be closest to the truth?

A seagull swoops close to the window. In my notebook I write:

> 10. Who's responsible for the story of my mom?

Memory.

The rocks rise in layers of gold beneath the sun. They've been shaped by the wind. Water has left its mark like trickles of dark blood. My mother disappears into the deep shadows beyond the sign that warns of falling rocks—I can only read the picture—and I want to follow her in but I'm scared. When I call her, the wind takes off with my words. I know there are places she goes to, parts of her, which I can't yet understand. I wait with the sun, for my mother to return.

LIFE IN A GLASSHOUSE

I FOUND A BOOK in the local library by a philosopher called Wittgenstein. I borrowed it because it's full of diagrams and equations, a language I know. The only problem is, Wittgenstein explains in the preface that he believes he has found the solution to the questions of philosophy, but that his book, he says, *shows how little is achieved when these problems are solved.*

Seb's sprawled on his bed, staring up at the ceiling, straight into Thom Yorke's eyes. Radiohead posters cover every surface in his room, except for a photo of him as a baby hung next to his door. He cut a deal with his mom—one baby shot against a roomful of posters. A T-shirt with the words *Insane citizen* printed on it in white is draped over the photo.

It's Tuesday after school. I have a shining desire to tell him about Taryn, but I hold back. Seb flops over the side of the bed and turns the volume on his stereo down from disfiguring to loud. "So, how is it at your place?"

"You mean with Adam home? Yeah, all right. You know how he is."

"Been giving you a hard time?"

"The usual."

He turns the music down even further. "Remember that time I stayed over at your place and he turned us in for stealing matches? Man, what an asshole. You know, I reckon Adam's always been jealous of you."

"Really?"

"Yeah, the way you were with your mom. Anyway, I thought he might go easier on you now, considering."

"I guess." I grab a comic from the pile on the floor, with a picture of some kind of mutant warrior on the front. Seb does comics, not me.

He rolls over onto his back. "I was talking to Mom about . . . about how I could help."

"Help?"

"I never had a friend whose mom died before."

"So, what did she say?"

His feet beat out a rhythm but it's not the same one as the music. The song's "Jigsaw Falling into Place." "She said that I should say that I'm sorry, about what happened. And that if there's anything you need I'm here."

"And what do you think?"

"I haven't got a clue."

Seb's waiting. I know all he wants is for me to say it's okay, that one day soon our old life will reassert itself, but I can't.

He heaves his hand through his hair. "I was trying to work out what I'd want you to do if Mom died, but every time I think about it I get this kind of buzzing in my head."

I look down at a drawing of a guy getting it in the neck with an ax. "When's she getting home?"

"Who? My mom? Not till after five. Why?"

I lean over and turn the music up, so loud it blocks out the possibility of thought.

On my way out, Seb's mom, Jackie, pulls into the driveway. She gets out of her car and her heel catches on a crack in the pavement. For a moment I think she's going to fall.

"Will, it's good to see you. How have you been?"

I thrust my hands deeper into my pockets. "Yeah, good, thanks."

"And your dad? Would it help if I brought over a lasagna?"

"It's okay. We're learning how to cook."

"I know I said it at your mom's funeral, but if there's anything I can do. Anything at all."

Her hand reaches out. I pull my school bag higher on my shoulder as her wedding ring catches the light and I want to slap her hand away and shout, *Well, yes, actually, why don't we do an exchange. I'll have my mother back, and Seb can be the poor kid without a mom.*

"Will?"

She touches my sleeve. The hairs stand up on my arms and my legs go limp. I'm going to drop right here on the driveway, a stretched-out pathetic heap, for the entire world to contemplate and come up with their own neat little theories on how it is we survive. Except I don't. I feel a resurrecting force instead, a pulse surging up from my feet, all the way to my head.

"I'm late," I say, and I go, down the driveway, past the oak tree that drops helicopters in autumn, all the way to the end of the street. And by the time I get there I'm running.

* * *

Memory.

My mother's necklace. A silver bell. It bangs against her chest as she moves. I lay my head on her breast and hold the bell up to the light, jingle it, listen to the tiny silver clapper as it hits the sides. It is the sound of sanctuary.

When I get home, nobody's there. I think about calling Taryn but go into my parents' room instead. The sun makes zebra stripes through the blinds across the bed.

I open the top drawer of the dresser. Everything is neatly sorted, though Mom was more a chuck-it-in-there type; *artistic with housework* she would say. I guess Dad's been tidying up. All her things—underwear, a drawer liner, socks. I pull the liner out and the scent of roses, suggested more by the design on the paper than any lingering smell, is enough to conjure that Saturday afternoon. The one when Dad took me shopping to buy her a present for her birthday. The indecision, the companionable secrecy, and then the next day the unreadable expression on her face as she opened the drawer liners, her cheeks still creased with sleep.

I slide the liner back, making sure it looks as if it's never been touched. The closet's open like a request—it's easy to tell which her things are, they're so much more colorful. I squat among the boxes and shoes, my head stuck in the hems and their scent. I slide my fingers under the door and drag it shut behind me. A strip of light bisects my knee. It is even quieter in here; all I can hear is my breath which sounds afraid of the dark, as if it's aware of the limited air inside the closet, of the finite number of breaths. My mother didn't get to breathe all of hers—somebody stole them from her. Somebody she'd never even met performed the ultimate theft, and yet he lives.

I try to remember his name. Dad told me it—I don't know how he knew, somehow he did that day at the hospital, the day they split her open to try and salvage her life. Connelly, maybe, or Conrad. I hope he's in a shitload of pain. I hope his hurting outstrips mine by a thousand lashes. That he has some awareness of what he's done, a tiny insight into the world he's created, and the one he took away.

In my bedroom, on a card Mom kept for thank-you notes I write a quote from *Macbeth*:

> *Taryn,*
>
> *The grief that does not speak whispers the o'erfraught heart and bids it break.*
>
> *Love,*
> *Will*

TWO

THE DANCE

FRIDAY NIGHT, we're invited to Taryn's again—I think she might have had something to do with it. We all go, even Adam, and both Taryn's sisters are home, so we can hardly fit into the living room as Ray shows us in. "Samara's just flown in from Pakistan."

"It was getting a bit dangerous, too many attacks," Samara says, smiling, her dark hair drawing a straggly line across her back.

"I'm Adam," he says, checking her out.

"We're just glad to have you back in one piece, love. And this is Frida." Frida reaches over and shakes our hands. Her hair is the same marmalade as Taryn's. "Frida works for a recruitment firm."

"Which one?" asks Adam, as Taryn edges over to me.

"Let's go," she whispers. Adam looks at us, at our linked fingers, but I don't flinch, not a muscle, till Taryn leads me away. In the kitchen, her bangs caught in her eyelashes, she says, "Thanks for the card."

I brush the stray hair out of her eyes, imagine entering in through them. God, I'd like to know what I feel like to her.

She smiles. "Give sorrow words."

"What?"

"It's the line before the quote you sent me, the one in the card about the overfraught heart. Give sorrow words." She presses her hand to my chest, the heat of it drawing out and dispelling something dark. "You can tell me anything, you know, anything at all."

I trace a pattern of freckles down to her lips. Kiss them. Let the scent of her wash over me as I absorb the promise in what she's said.

"I had a dream about you last night, Will."

"Oh, yeah."

"You were all golden, like that night out at the mandala, and . . ."

I want to touch the spot where the skin of her neck disappears into her dress.

"It was as if you had a thousand hands."

"A thousand hands?"

"Bit like Nataraja," says Samara, breaking in. "Sorry, guys, they were starting to talk real estate. Not my thing." She plonks down at the table.

"Who?" I ask, my eyes forced away from Taryn's neck.

"The Hindu god of creation and destruction," says Samara, an edge of pride in her voice. She's wearing a white dress which is heavily embroidered on the front. She sees me looking at it, and smiles. "A friend in Pakistan gave it to me. Bought it for me in Rawalpindi market."

"Is that where you learned about Hindus? In Pakistan?"

"No, most people there are Muslims, though I met some up in the mountains who believe in fairies."

"Fairies?"

"Yeah. Life-sized ones that live on glaciers." Samara twists the ring on her little finger around and around with her thumb. "Up there, there's still a fair bit of animist belief."

"So what's an animist when it's at home?" asks Adam as he comes in, followed by Frida.

So much for being alone.

Adam takes a lingering look at Taryn as he sits down at the table, next to the groove.

"An animist believes that everything has a soul. Rocks. Trees. Even people." Samara smiles at her audience, stretches her arms above her head. "Anybody want some wine?"

She fills five glasses from a bottle on the table while the rest of us sit down, Taryn and Samara on either side of me.

"So, do they believe that wine has a soul?" asks Adam, raising his glass like he's checking if one might be floating around in there. When he doesn't get an answer he tries again. "Done a bit of traveling in Asia myself."

"Oh, yeah," says Frida, smiling, sipping her wine. "Whereabouts?"

"Kuala Lumpur, Singapore, Bangkok. For business. Financing. Been doing it for three years now. Had enough of university, and Dad had this friend in Hong Kong who gave me a job."

"Lucky you," says Samara. "So, what happened at school?"

"Not good at sitting in a classroom, I guess."

Adam's watching Samara over the top of his glass but she turns to me. "What about you, Will?"

"Will's the smart one," says Adam. "When he was a kid he was more interested in world poverty than riding his bike."

"How about you let him answer for himself?"

I wait for Adam to pitch something back at her, but all he does is unfurl his hand in my direction. "Will?"

"I'm still studying," I say.

Taryn: "He's into philosophy."

"What about Eastern philosophy?" asks Samara. "Are you interested in that?"

"Don't know much about it."

I can almost hear Adam thinking, *Bunch of hippies*. He empties the last of the bottle into Samara's glass. "You girls sure can drink. Put me and Will to shame."

"Is he always such a prick?" Samara asks me with a grin, her shoulder touching mine. "Hey, remind me to give you something before you go, something I got in India."

She goes over to the wine rack on the bench and selects another bottle. Taryn's fingers seek out the inside of my leg.

"Christ, you wouldn't believe how much I missed a good glass of Aussie red while I was overseas," says Samara, looking at Adam, then back at me.

"Well, what are you waiting for?" he asks.

We're getting ready to go home when Samara says, "Hey, you two, come with me."

Taryn and I follow her to her room—it's next to Taryn's and it's like walking into a bazaar, purple and orange cloth suspended from the ceiling, strewn across the bed, embroidered cushions, statues, and incense, of course.

Taryn shuffles some cards she takes from a gold box as Samara hands me a statue of a dancing figure with four arms. It's heavy and made of brass. "This is Nataraja. I got him in Madurai, at a stall outside the temple. The temple's like a city, it's incredible. You should go there."

Madurai. Sounds like the kind of place where you could mislay yourself. Samara squats next to a shelf with books stacked in every direction. She's wearing purple nail polish and rings on her toes. I turn the statue around in my hands—there's a circle haloing the figure with brass flames flickering from its rim, a man squashed beneath Nataraja's feet, skulls woven into his hair.

"He's dancing the dance of creation and destruction. Nataraja is one of the incarnations of Shiva," says Samara, touching each book's spine as she checks its title. "He's the most powerful of the Hindu gods."

"How many have they got?"

"An old guy on a train to Calcutta told me there are as many gods in India as there are people, because we are all aspects of God. Here it is."

I put the statue back on top of the shelf, next to a pile of incense ash. She hands me a book. It has a green and orange cover and the title is in gold lettering, hard to read, so I hold it up to the light. *The Tibetan Book of Living and Dying.*

"I thought it might be appropriate," Samara says, "considering."

Before I can do anything, she puts her arms around my shoulders and gives me a hug. She's warm against me, rounder than Taryn, a different scent, earthier, and she feels like . . . God, such a strong urge to cry, and then that creepy feeling all over again.

Samara lets her hands slide down my arms as she pulls away. I grab Taryn's hand and go, the taste of all that incense sticking in my throat.

Dad and Adam are already in the car, the moon slapped across the windshield.

"She's beautiful," says Adam.

Tempted as I am, I don't ask him which one he means.

Will,

Sorry about Samara. She can be a bit much.

♥ Taryn

When I come in from the study, Dad's already gone to bed, but Adam's watching the late news. On the screen are scuttling images of men in camouflage and UN tanks. His head's tilted to the side as he watches, like Mom always did. She gave birth to us; we are the only two living creatures on this planet who can say that. We are united by her blood. Despite our age difference, he's always been a different kind of presence from Mom or Dad. But since he's been home, it's as if he's hovering somewhere in between—three generations living in this house of males.

A woman is holding her head and screaming at a pile of dust. The reporter, microphone in hand, leans into the camera and says it used to be her son and I have a sudden need to throw my arms around Adam and squeeze him hard, wring him until the mockery has oozed out of him and in its place there is only a quiet, honest response. To death. To love. To blood.

Adam grabs the remote and the TV goes dark.

KISS THE JOY AS IT FLIES

I KNOW NOTHING about Eastern philosophy, except that Buddha was a fat guy with a big grin. The book Samara gave me has words in it like *karma* and *bardos* and *samsara*, but I notice one thing straight off—the word *love*. In this book, everything has something to do with love. The man who wrote it, Sogyal Rinpoche, is a Buddhist master and was brought up by monks. They escaped from Tibet, went over the Himalayas into India. He's got a lot to say about death: *When I first came to the West . . . I learned that people today are taught to deny death, and taught that it means nothing but annihilation and loss . . . many people believe that simply mentioning death is to risk wishing it upon themselves.*

According to Sogyal Rinpoche, we love being busy so we don't have to think about our own mortality, about what's important, even what makes us happy. He calls it *active laziness*, which reminds me of what Seneca said about wasting your life.

The house is quiet. Saturday morning, everyone's sleeping in. I look at the pile on my bedside table—Seneca's book's still there, below a dictionary of philosophy I borrowed. The dictionary doesn't have a section on dying, or love.

I take another look at Rinpoche's book. *Modern society seems to me a celebration of all the things that lead away from the truth.* I pick up my notebook:

> *11. What if I don't have the ability to recognize the truth?*

Dad's in the laundry room, slouched against the washing machine. There's a mass of dirty clothes on the floor like a pile of dismembered limbs. I've come in to find some socks—we haven't quite got a handle on the washing thing yet. I squat down to pick through the pile, which is starting to fester.

"You all right, Dad?"

"We've run out of laundry detergent."

I point to the broom closet. "I think Mom kept it in there."

"I've tried to find it."

"Do you want me to have a look?"

He sounds annoyed. "No, I mean, in the shops. I've been to three supermarkets, none of them have it."

"Really?"

These two socks are close enough, nearly the same black. I pull them on but they don't smell so good. Lucky I'm not seeing Taryn today.

"I guess we'll have to change brands then," I say.

"No, we can't."

"What?"

I half expect him to laugh, but he doesn't, his forehead huddling down around his eyes. "If we use another detergent, we'll smell different."

* * *

I look the detergent up on the Internet and find a supplier. It's some special biodegradable stuff. I order two boxes of it with Dad's credit card.

The key to finding a happy balance in modern lives is simplicity.

Sogyal Rinpoche

Maybe we should dump the computers and go live in a tent in the bush.

T ♥

When do we leave?

"You serious?" Taryn asks, wrapping herself around me as we lie in the sun on the grass in her backyard on Monday afternoon.

"About what?"

"About taking off together."

"Sure."

She rolls up on top of me, nestles her hips into mine. "Imagine no one around to stop us when we want to have sex. Be nice, wouldn't it, out here in the sun?"

"Now?" I ask, slipping my hand up under her dress. Oh God, yes.

"Yes, now."

"But I don't have any condoms with me. And what if somebody sees us?"

"Do you care?" She kisses my neck, her breath already deepening.

The next-door house is higher than the fence and there are windows facing us. "Taryn?"

Her body goes limp in my hands. "I know, I know. God, you're so logical."

"Am I?"

She rolls off me. "Sometimes a little too much."

It's the first time she's ever said anything to me that felt like a punch. "Nothing wrong with a little discipline of the mind."

"Jesus. You've been reading that book of Samara's, haven't you?"

"So?"

"Be careful, that's all. If you read too much of that stuff it can warp your perception."

"Of what?"

"Life. What's important."

"I thought it was meant to help you focus on that kind of thing."

"I know, but it's all about the mind."

I pull her thigh into me, my finger fumbling over a scab. "What's this?"

She lifts her dress to show me. "I scratched myself on the bathroom vanity the other day. Do you think it'll scar?"

"Probably not. You'd still be . . ." I circle a freckle next to it while the words work up the courage. "You'd still be beautiful if it did."

"Beautiful, you reckon?"

"Sure, even with a huge scar."

Taryn whacks me on the arm and laughs. I stare up at the

sky, at the day moon pale against it, my finger fascinated by her scab.

"What are you thinking?" she asks.

"About how we are constantly losing our skin, our hair, our blood. I mean, in forty years from now I won't even be the same person, at least on a molecular level."

"Yeah, but that's not all we are, is it?"

"No, not only."

"Well, what else then?"

"I was thinking that even our minds change constantly. The way I think has changed since . . ."

"Since you met me?"

"Yeah," I say, although I was thinking *since Mom died.* "I mean, it's weird. Why are we so afraid of dying, when we're losing bits of ourselves all the time?"

"Maybe it's because it's only when we lose something suddenly that we notice," she says. "We don't see the small deaths. Though, I believe some part of you never dies."

Moon behind her head, she smiles at me with the kind of certainty that eclipses all doubt. I slide my hands under her dress and roll her over onto her back as our mouths converge.

When I get home, I find one of Taryn's hairs, long and golden and straight, caught under my arm. I wind it into a spiral, put it in a piece of folded paper, and stow it in the box under my bed. A small piece of her.

In *The Tibetan Book of Living and Dying,* Rinpoche says that there are two layers to the mind—the first is like a candle by an open door and every time a breeze blows in, the flame moves, in the same way our thoughts are affected by what's happening around us, someone pissing you off, falling in love. But deep down is our other mind, something far more constant, though we hardly ever notice that it exists. There are times when we get a glimpse of it, an inkling of how we could be.

I remember sitting at the edge of a huge rock face up in the mountains, the day in the photos Mom took. I could see for miles, the wind fanning smells from below—eucalyptus, a distant bushfire—and I had this feeling, like belonging to everything, like truly seeing myself, and at that very moment, I swear, I felt happy to die. Not some wrist-slashing thing, more an intense longing to leap. And then it was gone, and I recoiled from the edge, my whole body caught in this kind of vertigo, except I've never been afraid of heights. Adam came up behind me as I staggered: *You were a little close to the edge there, buddy. Thought for a minute you were going to jump. Lucky Mom didn't see you, she would've freaked.*

Mom was there, somewhere farther back along the track. She looked like she'd live forever as she unpacked the ham sandwiches onto the picnic table, white bread for Dad and Adam, whole wheat for us. But she only had half a year to live.

Two seasons.

She would never see autumn again.

And what would I have said to her that afternoon, if I'd known that she'd soon be dead? Something about love? I like to think I would have made sure that every moment counted, because it was bringing us closer to our last.

I reach over and pull a book out from the pile beside my lamp. It's a collection of poems by William Blake we've been studying in Lit and there's one I have a sudden need to read. I flick through the pages, past the "Songs of Innocence" and "Songs of Experience," until I find what I'm looking for. I go into the study and send Taryn this:

Hey beautiful,

He who binds himself a Joy,
Does the winged life destroy;
He who kisses the Joy as it flies,
Lives in Eternity's sunrise.

William Blake

♥ Will

Let's be like that, Will. Let's kiss the joy as it flies.

♥ T

BY THE WORLD FORGOT

A WOMAN'S LAUGHTER WAKES ME. And there's music. My legs take a while to obey me. It's cold out of bed. There's a sapphire light coming from the living room, like some alien invasion, but no laughter anymore. Adam's sitting on the couch, his face blue.

"Hey. What're you watching?"

"*The Eternal Sunshine of the Spotless Mind.*"

He hands me the cover. On the front, there's a man lying next to a woman with blue hair, on cracked ice. I collapse on the couch next to Adam. He's wearing pajama pants, his face transfixed, the sinews on his arms defined by the blue light. The guy in the movie has just discovered that targeted memory erasure is possible, at least in his world. Adam shifts his eyes to me. "Mom lost a baby."

"What?"

"Between you and me. That's why there's such a big gap between us."

His face returns to the screen. The guy's collecting up all the mementos that might remind him of the woman with the blue hair, the memory he wants to erase. He's filled two green garbage bags. The doctor in the movie's saying that *there's an emotional core to each of our memories.* That the erasure will feel like *a dream upon waking.*

"How come you know this and I don't?"

"I remember it. Dad took care of me for weeks. I think she was pretty sick."

Adam hugs his knees into himself, and reaches for the blanket at the end of the couch. The guy's wearing some bizarre kind of memory recording device, like an old-fashioned hair dryer. It's meant to make a map of his brain so that they find the right memories to erase. The guy is focused on the woman, remembering her, in all her beauty and her fury, in order to forget.

"Was it a boy or a girl?"

"Don't know."

Adam tucks the blanket under his feet, the light flickering on his face. Mom always wanted a girl. If she'd had one, I might never have been born. Even conceived. Would they have called it Will if it was a boy?

> *The world forgetting, by the world forgot.*
> *Eternal sunshine of the spotless mind!*
>
> —Alexander Pope

The shopping mall's out of control, too many kids throwing tantrums, women asserting themselves with strollers. Dad's given me money to get new jeans. I buy some sushi, chicken teriyaki, and at one of the long, slatted tables I mix plenty of wasabi into the soy. A woman storms past with three kids. One, a small boy in an Incredible Hulk T-shirt, trails behind, then halts in front of a baby shop. A huge blue teddy is on display, guarding a stroller that looks like it could take you to the moon. I had a brother or sister who died two years before I was born. Adam remembers Mom being pregnant, the swelling of her stomach, his own ambivalent thoughts. The void when Mom was gone.

"Aidan. Hurry up!"

It's the kid's older sister, hands on hips. Next to the baby shop, a guy wearing a baseball cap shoves money into a drinks machine, but it goes straight through. He keeps collecting the rejected coins, thrusting them in the slot, over and over. He should be careful—more people get killed by vending machines falling on them than are eaten by sharks. And that kid, Aidan. What's going to happen to him—will he drown in their pool one day when his big sister isn't watching, or make it to ninety-five and croak in his sleep? All these people, every one of them, will one day no longer exist.

The roof in this place is high, like a cathedral, but the whole feel is artificial. It's easy to imagine it empty, filled only with the ghosts of things—naked mannequins, empty hangers, vacant tills—and, hovering somewhere up near the ceiling, the memory of all these people that in one hundred years from now will be gone.

I separate my chopsticks with a snap, dip the sushi into the sauce, shove it whole into my mouth, my nostrils flaring, the wasabi's so hot. I love when that happens, it makes me feel clean, like all the crap's been seared out of my brain. It allows room for clear thought, a whole new range of questions.

12. How will I die?

Memory.

My pop's dead. He had bowel cancer. I'm six. I think about how he always slipped me an extra scoop of ice cream when Nan wasn't looking, and how his arms looked like lizard skin. I thought he was some kind of reptile till Mom said he wasn't—I remember she didn't laugh when she explained this to me.

I find my mother crying in different parts of the house. She keeps a hanky in her pocket and, when I draw it out and hand it to her, she asks me if there's anything I want to say. I think for a minute before I answer, "Don't worry, Mommy, he'll be back for Christmas. Who else will hand out the presents?" My mother absorbs her tears and stows her hanky away.

Christmas comes, but no Pop. Nobody mentions him; Dad hands out the presents instead. I get a huge truck from my nan but, when nobody's looking, I take it outside and bury it in the sandpit. Nan gives me an extra scoop of ice cream, even though I don't finish my lunch.

CELEBRATION

TOMORROW WOULD HAVE BEEN my mother's fifty-second birthday. It is five weeks since she died.

Over noodles, which Adam cooked, which aren't half bad, I make a suggestion. "I think we should celebrate Mom's birthday. Go out for a meal."

Dad: "Adam, what do you think?"

Adam, chopsticks poised, takes a sip of his beer. I get ready for him to shred my idea. "Sure. What about that Thai place in the shopping strip. I'll call and book if you like."

So, maybe I do believe in miracles.

"Thai. Sounds good. All right with you, Will?"

"All right with me, Dad."

The two of them go back to their noodles. The only sound, the click of chopsticks as they tap the insides of their bowls.

There are heaps of kids at the restaurant so it's raucous, but the smell wafting from the kitchen reminds me how much I love Thai. A woman the size of a child shows us to our seats.

"Looks good," says Adam, checking out the menu. "Been a

while since I had a good pad thai. Got sick of the stuff in Bangkok, but now I kind of miss it." He's being so cheerful I wonder what he's saving up.

"I don't want anything too hot," says Dad. "I think I'll go for the tom yum soup. Nice place, Adam."

The waitress yanks the cork out of our bottle of wine; it takes most of her strength.

"Guess it won't hurt," says Dad as she fills my glass, "you're almost eighteen. Here's to . . ." He pauses, like he's forgotten something.

"Here's to Mom," I say.

"To Anna."

"To Mom," says Adam under his breath.

Dad smiles, runs his finger around the base of his wineglass. "This guy at work, John Braithewaite . . . Will, I think you met him at the staff picnic."

"The short guy who kept making jokes about penguins?" I grin.

"Yes, that's him. He's just found out he's got cancer. They've given him three months to live, poor guy. He's only forty-two."

Adam's been making some sort of origami with his napkin, but he looks up now. "This was meant to be a celebration. Can't we talk about something else?"

"Adam's afraid that if we mention death we'll bring it on."

"That's not funny."

"Wasn't meant to be."

Dad: "Keep your voice down, Adam."

I take a deep breath. "So, why did you decide to move back after Mom died?"

"You looking for a confession?"

"No. Just a little truth."

"We don't all have to be like you, Will, analyzing everything to crap."

Dad cuts in: "Adam, that's enough."

"I'm just sick of him . . ."

"I said that's enough! Whether you like it or not, this is Will's way of dealing with what happened to your mom."

Adam's frown morphs into a smile as he turns to me. "And don't think you'll find the meaning of life in some book Samara gave you. She's such a bloody cliché, with her Indian clothes. The only place you'll find truth in that house is between Taryn's legs."

"You asshole," I spit. I want to crush him, splinter that grin on his face.

"Either you apologize, Adam, or you leave," says Dad, a fist tightening around his napkin.

"It's about time somebody told him a few home truths," Adam sneers and stands up. I stand too, taller than him, feeling the flow of anger course down the back of my hands.

"Is everything okay?" It's the miniature waitress standing between us with the bottle of wine.

"Fantastic," glares Adam as he leaves, knocking his napkin to the floor.

Dad bends down to pick it up but the waitress beats him to it. She pats it as she lays it on the table in front of Dad.

"It's not easy for him, but there's no excuse for acting that way. You okay, Will?"

"I could kill him . . ."

"Yeah, well, let's not ruin a good evening," he says, folding Adam's napkin, following the original creases, a man trying to make order of things, and I feel something slipping away from us so I grab at it before it's too late. "Dad?"

"Yes, Will?"

"What's the worst thing about Mom dying?"

For a moment it's like I haven't spoken, but he looks up from the fresh wine stain he's been running his finger over. "That I didn't die first."

Dad drinks too much so I drive, even though it's not allowed. The moon has an anemic glow that taints the stars. Adam doesn't come home.

After what happened at the restaurant last night, Taryn and I take refuge on her bed. Nobody else is home. "How could that guy be your brother?"

"Yeah, sometimes I wonder myself."

"I bet he's jealous he's got no one to love him."

It's been a while since Adam had a girlfriend as far as I know. He had one at the university though he never brought her home.

Taryn straddles me. "You know, I can't imagine not being with you."

"Things change," I say.

"I know that, Will."

Her knees nudge my ribs as she changes position.

"Sorry. Not much of a romantic, am I?"

"I think you are, but not in the usual way," she says, her finger settling on my lip. "There are plenty of ways to love."

Adam doesn't come home for two days, no phone call, nothing. I'm in the kitchen cooking dinner Saturday evening, when he finally gets back. "Where've you been?"

"At a friend's place."

"You could've called."

"Could've."

"Bit adolescent, don't you think?"

Adam gets a beer out of the fridge, twists the top off and chucks it at the small garbage can on the counter near the stove. It misses. I reach over and throw it in. "Didn't know you could cook curry," he says.

"Taryn showed me how." I give him a warning look.

He goes back to the fridge and takes out a second beer, opens it and hands it to me. I take a swig. "Well, just make sure it's good and hot."

"Dad doesn't like it spicy."

"Dad doesn't like anything spicy. A little change won't kill him."

"Maybe not." The smell of the curry reminds me of Taryn's house and I smile to myself.

"I know what you're thinking," says Adam, his lip a skeptical curl.

"I doubt that." I turn the gas down on the curry. "Can I show you something?"

"Sure, as long as it's not tarot cards."

I laugh. For some reason I'm immune to him tonight. "It's in my room."

Adam follows me, carrying both our beers. "What you got hiding in there?"

"Sit down," I say, pulling the box out from under my bed. "I found it in Mom's stuff."

Adam drops down next to me on the bed, moving a pile of books to the side. "If Dad catches you . . ."

"He won't."

The photo I hand him is in black and white, a close-up. It's of Adam and me—I'm a baby so Adam must be about six. He's holding me in his arms, looking at me like I'm the most beautiful thing he's ever seen. He taps the photo with his finger. "I remember this."

"I found it with a bunch of old letters."

Adam glances at me.

"I didn't read them. It was wrapped up in this." I let a blue silk scarf fall from my hand to his. He holds it up like an artifact.

"I've never seen the scarf before, but this photo, it's the day of your christening."

"I was christened? Nobody ever tells me anything."

"It's probably the only time you've been in a church."

I think to tell him about the day in St. Paul's with the candles, and that time with Mom, but I don't want to sidestep his thoughts.

Adam smiles. "The priest, when he sprinkled the water over your head, you gave him this filthy look. I swear. I remember being proud of you. I remember thinking, this baby is my brother. It was kind of weird—I'd waited a long time to get one, especially after Mom lost the other baby." He wraps the photo back in the scarf. "You know, we need to keep an eye on Dad. He's been working too hard."

"Active laziness."

"What?"

"Nothing. Yeah, I guess you're right. Maybe we could do something together. Something fun. Not like the other night."

"Yeah, sorry about that. I'd had a shit of a day."

"Jealousy's a curse," I say, looking at him sideways as I sip from my bottle.

He frowns, and then he gets it. "You talking about Taryn?" He shoves me hard, but he's laughing. I slam him back, nearly push him off the end of the bed. He barely manages to save his beer.

"We could all go away, maybe for a weekend? Go camping," I say.

"You mean, do a little male bonding?"

"Jesus, Adam, can't you drop the sarcasm for once?"

He grins. "If you insist. God, it's been ages since I went camping."

"Dad always liked it, remember, it was kind of our thing."

"As long as you're sure you can bear to be away from Taryn."

"For Christ's sake."

"No, I'm serious," he says. "I remember what it's like. You two seem pretty close."

"Yeah, we are."

"So, stop moping around trying to solve the problems of the universe. Enjoy what you've got."

"Yeah, maybe you're right," though there's something about the word *moping* that pisses me off.

"I know I am. You want another beer? Dad won't be home for a while. Anyway, these days I don't think he'd care."

"Sure." I put the photo back in the box as Adam gets up. He's wearing a new pair of trousers with a sharp crease down each leg; he must've bought them while he was gone. "Adam?"

"Yeah?"

"Do you reckon everything's going to be all right?"

Memory.

Adam and me having a fight. I'm about seven, Adam thirteen. He's got me against the wall and he's shouting, "Shut up!" He wants to hurt me, I can see it in his face, the way his lip curls.

Mom steps up beside us, says, "Adam, let go." The tremble of his hand as he grips my shirt and stares at her. "Let go," she repeats, "that's Will's way. He's different from you." "He's crazy," my brother says. He lowers his face close to mine and releases me, strides off in disgust. My mother's arms circling me.

WHISPER

THE GIRL AT THE COUNTER is wearing a fluorescent green T-shirt and a nose ring that sparkles as her nostrils flare. Some bald man's looking for an opera CD she's obviously never heard of and she's giving him her best get-lost grin. Seb's in the Goth metal section, next to a guy who clanks when he walks. It's like a fancy dress party in here. I pull my jacket around my uniform and head for the Bs.

They're playing Disturbed over the system and it's good and loud. I find B and start sorting through the discs—there's a lot of shit in here—and then I find what I'm looking for.

"What's that?" asks Seb, like I'm holding a dead baby in my hand.

"Jeff Buckley. A live recording."

"Jeff Buckley? Are you kidding?"

"It's not for me."

I can see the frown behind his veil of hair. "Who's it for, then?"

"This girl I know."

"Which girl?"

"Her name's Taryn. I met her at my mother's wake."

"That's weird."

"Well, actually I saw her there . . . doesn't matter."

"She's got crap taste in music, whoever she is."

I put the CD back in its place. "She's got long hair," I add. Like that explains everything.

"Oh, yeah."

"And her parents used to be friends with mine."

This isn't getting closer to anything. He's waiting for more, but I don't know what to say, we don't do these kinds of conversations. Seb's bangs stick in his eyes as he shakes his head. "You're having sex with her, aren't you?"

I pick the Jeff Buckley CD up again and push the rest of the row back. The sound of plastic on plastic, an urge to smile that I resist.

"Shit," he says, folding his arms across his chest. "Are you in love, or something?"

"Yeah, maybe I am."

"Well, okay," he says, scooping his bangs out of his eyes. Then he heads for the counter where the bald guy seems to be miming the opera, the girl with the nose ring having lost the will to live.

That night, I wrap Taryn's CD in some purple paper I find in the linen closet where Mom kept all the birthday stuff. Apart from the fridge, my sounds are the only ones in the house. Everyone else is asleep. Adam came home early and had dinner with us, spaghetti carbonara, which Dad cooked. Dad's getting the hang of it, I think he even enjoys it, except when he pulls something out of the cupboard that nobody's touched since Mom died. This evening, when it happened, he turned the jar of peppercorns around in his hands as if he was jealous of its last contact.

There's no moon so I rely on body memory to find my way back to my room, but as I go past Dad's half-open door, I hear a noise. Edging closer, I recognize his voice. I can't quite make out what he's saying—*cat*, maybe, or *cut*, but then, I'm sure of it, I hear the word *will*. Or *Will*.

My father rolls over onto his back. He's talking to Mom. "What would you do?" he whispers into the dark.

Silence.

I want to thrust the door wide open, tell him that I'm okay, that he only needs to take care of himself.

"Fuck!"

The word cuts through the stillness of the house. Dad rolls over again and I hear him punch into a pillow. "Fuck, fuck, fuck." I close my eyes, press into the wall, don't breathe until the punching stops. One last drawn out "fuuuck," followed by a long groan.

I want to go to him, but don't. Back in my room, I draw my sheet over my face.

IF WATER HAD MEMORY

CHEMISTRY. The investigation of matter and the substances of which it is composed. Such as alcohol, which is what we're meant to be distilling, except Henkel went to get some papers she'd been grading, so nothing's happening. Standard Tuesday afternoon in Chem. Seb's lending his earphones to Rick, "the dick," or "prick," depending on who you are.

Henkel comes in. "Class!"

Rick spins around, wires dangling from his ears, and knocks the burner over. Splintering glass. Water and alcohol everywhere.

"Shit," says Henkel, racing over.

"Yeah, shit," I say, as she goes past.

"Stand back, everyone." She frowns at me as she turns the burner off and points to Rick. "You can clean this up. The rest of you get on with the experiment. Will, can you come up here for a minute?"

Rick rolls his eyes at me. Definitely "prick." I go up to Henkel; her lab coat has a green ink stain on the pocket the shape of a squashed pear.

"Will. You've always been a good student . . ."

"What?" Arms crossed, I lean against the whiteboard, as she pushes her glasses higher on her nose. They never stay up on their own.

"Mr. McKinley explained about your mother."

"Oh, yeah. So what did he explain?"

"Well, that she died."

"I see. And did he give you any details? For example, that she was hit by a red Honda? Or that they cut her chest open to try and revive her even though she was technically dead?"

She looks down at the papers covered in red marks, and takes her glasses off. She has nice eyes. "Will. I don't think this is very helpful."

"No? Well, *I* think you can go and get fucked." And before she can say anything, I go, down the deserted corridor, past the Year 12 lockers and out into the rain, and I keep going, across the muddy oval and over the fence, till my shoes are squelching and I'm soaked.

In an empty bus shelter not far from the supermarket, I sit and shiver. Cars, trucks, bikes plummet past, tires flicking up the rain. God, I hope a bus doesn't come along, I can't do people right now. Though, if one does, maybe I'll get on it, see where it takes me. Far away. Anywhere but here.

When I get home, I strip, climb in the bath, slide beneath the surface of the water and hold my breath. Everything is amplified, the squeak of my ass against the porcelain walls, distant hollow sounds as I try to stay under, but it's too warm, I can't. Before my lungs start to scream, I drag myself above the surface of the water. And for the hell of it, I fart.

* * *

I saw this program on TV tonight, before I went to bed. They were talking about water having memory. Most of your body is made up of water, they said, a constant process of evaporation and reabsorption: from the tap, moisture in the air, recycled sweat. Maybe that's why old couples start to look like each other—they keep exchanging carbon and H_2O. Like us. Adam, Dad, and me.

I drag my arm out from under the sheet and turn it around in front of my face. Part of me used to be my brother, another used to be Mom. There has been an exchange. Some of my molecules went with her and now they lie unraveling in the earth. That's if they were ever really mine.

While I watched that show I thought about what kind of memory water might hold. Maybe somewhere deep down I have memories of being a watermelon or a fish. Then I got to thinking that maybe this is what Buddhists mean about being born over and over again. And every now and then you get a glimpse: you remember what it's like to be part of the sea.

I get out of bed, stand in front of the mirror naked, tall, scrawny, in need of a tan. My hair a bit anarchic, a birthmark like a tear on my left hip, my dick hanging there like some forlorn thing. So this is me, Will Ellis, this is my part of the world. I raise my arms above my head, wave them around—shit, I hope Adam doesn't come in. The more I analyze myself, the more I feel detached. My body has disconnected from the flow of the world.

I touch the mirror but it's cold, so I concentrate on my hand instead, run my fingers over the skin with its tiny crevices, the knuckles, my nails where they go from white to pink. The palm with its lines, one of which is supposed to reveal your destiny, but I don't know which one it is. Not sure I'd want to. These are my hands but it's as if they belong to somebody else.

I close my eyes, put my hands over my face, hear my breath going into them, feel the moisture in it. There's memory held there. If I were to stop breathing now, because that's all it takes, isn't it, the stopping of breath? One lifetime extinguished. So fragile. If I were to stop, my body would drop to the floor, and I'd still seem the same for a while, as if asleep. I can imagine it if I concentrate, and visualize my body slumped on the floor, as if every part of me has been waiting all this time to become part of everything else, to remember what it once was.

13. Do my mother's memories live in me?

ARROWS AND MAXIMS

I'M WRAPPED NAKED AROUND Taryn when we hear someone in the house.

"Who is it?" I whisper, grabbing for my clothes.

"Probably Samara. Mom and Dad aren't due home for ages." She snatches at my T-shirt, tosses it back on the floor. "Don't worry, she won't care."

There's a knock followed by Samara's gravelly voice. "You there, Taryn?"

"Yeah, I'm with Will."

"I'll come back later, if you like."

"No, it's all right, you can come in." I raise my eyebrows at Taryn but all she does is laugh. "She knows we're having sex, for God's sake. Don't be so shy."

I make sure I'm covered as Samara comes in and sits on the end of the bed, her eyes roving over my bare chest.

"Got off work early and thought you might like to go for a swim. I'm going down to the lake."

"Samara's just got a job at a Nepalese restaurant," says Taryn, sitting up. The duvet falls to her waist. I want to lift it up and cover her but I know it will only make them laugh.

"It's only until I can get enough money together to hit the road again. What about going down to the lake?"

"The water'll be a bit cold, won't it?" says Taryn.

"Maybe," Samara says, "but it's so hot and I'm dying for a swim."

"What do you reckon, Will?"

"Sure. Missing a few more hours of study isn't going to make a difference. Anyway, it's Friday."

"I'll be in the kitchen making us something to eat," says Samara, getting up. "By the way, I've got a present for you, Will."

She leaves the door open, but Taryn pulls me down on top of her, wrestles her legs around me. "Pity we can't go skinny-dipping. Now that would be fun."

She feels so right against me, her mouth, her thighs, the life in her skin. And those eyes. She lets me look into them, doesn't flinch, until we both crack up.

"Get dressed, lover boy," she says, almost pushing me onto the floor.

The breeze off the lake is liberating after the heat. Taryn heads straight for the water as soon as she's stripped. Samara has a book of quotes by the Dalai Lama for me. "Aphorisms," she says.

"Aphorisms?"

"You know, short statements that say something profound."

I think Samara's decided she's my guru—she'll be asking me

for ten percent of my income soon, which from lawn mowing isn't that much. "Oh, yeah, I just didn't know that's what they're called. Wittgenstein used to write them. And Nietzsche. I remember seeing some in one of his books."

"Nietzsche. Talk about depressing. I tried reading him, can't remember which book of his it was. What an elitist prick. If you ask me, Western philosophy is too much in love with logic. No heart."

"You reckon?"

"Absolutely. There's no mystery, no place for what can only be felt."

"So, what about, *I would only believe in a God that knows how to dance*?"

"Now, that I like. Who said it?"

"Nietzsche."

"You're kidding me. Still reckon he was an elitist prick. You coming?"

"In a minute."

Samara pulls off her dress, straight over her head. I guess some things are genetic. She's wearing a blue bikini and she's tanned. Her belly button is pierced. The wind's forming patterns over the lake. Except for a family down at the other end of the beach, we're the only ones here. The kids are digging a huge hole, three of them working together like a mini construction company. Their mother is stretched out on a towel reading a book. Can't see what it is from here.

I pick up the collection of aphorisms, small and square-shaped, drop it open randomly to see what I find: *Peace won't come from the sky.*

I look up at the concentrated blue, almost purple. The clouds are like scrawled statements above the lake. There's a rim of scraggy eucalyptus trees around its edge. Taryn's waving to me from the tannin-stained water, her body hidden to the waist. She blows me a kiss. Only Samara's head is visible, already far out on the lake.

I close the book, check there's nothing in the pockets of my shorts, and then I go for it, straight down the beach, my feet shoveling back the sand, smashing through the water, body arched into a dive—that perfect instant before impact—the water cold as I enter it, cold enough to remind me who I am.

That evening, in my notebook, next to a quote from Wittgenstein, I write:

APHORISMS
by Will Ellis

[1]
To open your eye is to risk getting something in it.

[2]
A dead leaf is still a leaf.

[3]
A bird cannot fly without ruffling a few feathers.

[4]
You're unlikely to find a person's
heart between their legs.

[5]
The dead belong to the living.

[6]
Bird shit often contains seeds.

Memory.

I'm sitting on Mom's knee, her arms around my shoulders, my legs reach only halfway to the ground. She's telling me a story about an old man sowing seeds in his field and I like the way she's touching my hair. "It's a story from the Bible," she says, "it's called a parable. It's meant to explain things." I touch her face, feel the tiny hairs above her lip, see the light coming out of her eyes. As she continues her story about the old man and the seed, I let my cheek fall against her chest.

On my way to breakfast the next morning, I see Adam in the living room by the wall unit, staring at a photo of Mom. His body is bowed into it; he doesn't see me.

Saturday night, Taryn and I go and see *Casablanca*—she's into old films. In the café after the movie, I show her the aphorisms I wrote in my notebook. She likes the one about opening your eyes.

"I might have a go at writing some," she says.

"There's something I like about them."

"Me too, except they're a bit of a cop-out."

"What do you mean?"

"Well, it's a nice idea that you can explain things in the space of a few words. But you can't, of course."

She takes my pen and begins doodling a star on her paper napkin. I look at the posters on the walls, a mix of old and new films. A few of the titles read like aphorisms or quotes, one I recognize from *Macbeth*: *The Sound and the Fury.* I skim the foam off my hot chocolate. "It would be nice though if you could find the answer to every question in a single line. One truth that you could cling to. Or a piece of it, at least."

Taryn holds up the napkin. Next to the star and a chocolate stain, she's written: *Run naked through your fears.*

Seb's composing his favorite sandwich—it has everything in it that could conceivably be found between two slices of bread. He's invited me over to listen to the CD of *The Anatomy of Melancholy* he bought last Monday, the day I confessed.

"So what did you do on the weekend?" he asks, swallowing. "I called but your dad said you were out with Taryn."

"Yeah, we went to see a movie. And I'm not telling you which one."

"Fair enough." He offers me a bite of his sandwich. I decline. "Mom said you did a runner last time you were here."

"Yeah, well, couldn't stand the sympathy."

"She does that sometimes. She's just worried about you, that's all. Thinks you should be seeing someone."

"I am." I smile. "I'm seeing Taryn."

"You know what I mean." He goes to the pantry and gets a handful of Coco Pops and crunches them into his sandwich. "There's a party, Friday night, at Ritchie's. You going?"

"Don't know. Friday night, Taryn and me are . . ."

"What? Going to a yoga class?"

"Watch it!"

Seb chews his sandwich, his features focused around his mouth. He swallows. "Maybe you should take it slowly."

"What? With Taryn?"

"Yeah. I mean . . ."

"Since when were you the expert on women? Jesus, you've never even been laid."

"Neither had you till about a month ago, so, don't go pulling that crap on me. Anyway, Mom reckons it's a bit dangerous getting involved with someone so soon after your mother died."

"Well, that's just crap!"

Seb's face wedges into a frown. "She was only trying to help."

"Look, I'm fine, all right. So you can tell her not to worry."

"You're fine, are you?" he says, bits falling out of his sandwich. "Then what happened with Henkel the other day? You never did shit like that before."

"People change."

"Not that fast. I hardly recognize you . . . you're . . ."

"What?"

"All over the place."

"Why? Because I gave Henkel a hard time, and I've got a girlfriend?"

"No, it's more than that. You can't see it, but I do. It's like . . ."

"What, Seb? You jealous, or something?"

"It's like you're angry at me, at the whole universe, because your mom died, and I get that . . ."

"Oh, you do, do you?" I shift my weight as he puts his sandwich on the counter. "What do you want me to do? Pretend she never died?"

"Of course not."

"You know you can't just fix this with some ideas you've discussed over dinner with your mom."

"Will." Seb's hand is up in front of him like a surrender as he moves closer, and for a second I think . . .

"Don't you touch me."

"I wasn't . . ."

"God, I am so sick of people . . ."

"Trying to help?"

"Trying to tell me how I should be doing this."

There's a divisive silence. Seb moves toward me again.

"Don't, just, don't," I say. My heel collides with the table. "Shit!"

And then for the second time in a month I leave that house at a sprint, and I don't stop until my chest is pumping so hard my throat starts to ache. I lean forward onto my knees, try to take hold of my breath, even though I sense I'm not done with running yet.

Mom's photo's gone from the wall unit. Adam doesn't come home for dinner. Dad cooks pasta and manages to burn the sauce. My favorite Paradise Lost T-shirt gets mangled in the washing machine.

Will, don't forget the party at Ritchie's Friday. I'll be there. Bring Taryn. Seb

---

In my notebook I write:

[7]
If life could be explained in one sentence, it would contain no words.

MANTRA

"WILL YOU TEACH ME TO MEDITATE?"

"Sure," says Samara, looking at Taryn over the top of her glass of mint tea. "I've never taught anyone before, but if you're interested, Will, then you need to know about it."

With all this chaos, what I need is something to calm my mind. "When?"

"How about tomorrow afternoon? I'm not working till six."

Taryn pivots on my leg. Her bony butt is digging into my thigh. "But Wednesday I've got my dance class."

"Exactly. He can't learn with you around."

Taryn has her back to me so I can't see her face, but I feel her body shift. She turns and whispers in my ear, "Am I distracting you from your spiritual journey?"

Not a serious bone in her body.

"Around 4:30 tomorrow, then?" asks Samara.

I go to answer but Taryn's mouth is pressed against mine, her lashes against my cheek. Right now leaving my body behind is the furthest thing from my thoughts.

* * *

Samara's wearing tight tracksuit pants and a tank top when she opens the door. "Come in."

"Thanks," I say, but it feels wrong to be here without Taryn.

"I was thinking we should go out onto the back veranda. There's more space."

"I thought you closed your eyes to meditate."

"You do, but it'll help you settle yourself before we start."

There are two cushions on the deck, some incense burning, and I'm beginning to wonder why I came.

"It's nag champa," she says, "the best stuff for meditating. Take your shoes and socks off, you'll be more relaxed."

So I do, then sit on a cushion cross-legged like her. It's warm on the veranda, the smell of the garden mixing with the incense. I wait for my hay fever to kick in.

"So, first you put your hands like this." Samara balances a hand on each knee, palm up. "Then you touch the thumb and the index finger together. It's supposed to help with your breathing." Her voice has lowered. "Breathing's really important to meditation."

I put my hands like her on my knees and try to keep a straight face, like I'm a five-year-old, or something. As I remember, I was the one who asked her to do this.

"Okay, so now you close your eyes, and you focus your mind on the end of your nose, as if it's stroking the side of it, down to the tip."

I try to imagine it, my mind doing what she says. There's a warm, tingling sensation along my nose. I open my eyes; Samara's eyes are closed.

"Now, I want you to feel your breath as it enters through your nose, and I want you to take it up to your third eye."

She opens her eyes. "Sorry, I should have explained a few things before we started. Your third eye is in the middle of your forehead. It's the eye of your mind. Imagine that you are taking your breath up here." She touches her forehead. "Then you take the breath down to the base of your spine. That's where your life force is. The *kundalini*."

"Okay." I nod, feeling I should be taking notes. There's a resistance in me that I can't quite fathom.

"So, first you focus on the end of your nose, and then you take your breathing up to the third eye and down to the base of your spine. And, as you breathe, you say to yourself, *so hum*. That's a mantra—it helps focus the mind. If you're really focused, you'll see the color blue."

I do what she says, concentrate on the end of my nose, on the breathing, where it should go, what I'm meant to be saying in my head, as I feel my breath deepen. And then somebody shouts in another backyard. I open my eyes, but Samara hasn't noticed; her chest is still. I try to start again with the whole sequence, but the noises of the neighborhood keep dropping in on my mind.

"If you get distracted," she says, "start at the beginning. It takes practice."

I close my eyes again; nose, breath, base of the spine.

"Try and find that quiet place in your heart."

For a moment I do, but in my heart is Taryn, those freckles, the way her hair flirts as she moves. It's no use. I open my eyes but Samara is in meditation, her body inert, her face like Taryn's around the mouth, her breasts bigger. She's not as thin as Taryn—not fat, just more curved. Her eyes are shut and I study her freely—the bow of her hips, her bare feet, the crease between her legs. What the hell am I doing? I'm in love with Taryn and here I am weighing up the shape of Samara's tits. How can you love someone and lust after someone else? Because I do. I'm imagining Samara naked, right now, on the veranda, in that same position. My girlfriend's sister. Talk about taming the mind—obviously mine's a lot more feral than I thought. I'm all body, no control.

Samara takes a deep breath. "And when you've finished, you bring your hands over your head into the prayer position, and you bring them down in front of your body like this."

I do what she says. She opens her eyes, and smiles.

"Don't worry, the first few times your mind wanders all over the place. It's normal. Sometimes it can bring up the weirdest thoughts. You have to learn to calm it."

Well, that's the theory. I try to look innocent, she's being so nice, so like Taryn. I do my best to keep my eyes on her face.

"You okay, Will? It wasn't too strange for you, was it? The first time, it can be. If you're not used to the third eye thing, and all that."

"No, it was fine, really. Thanks."

Except it wasn't. All this shit is starting to unhinge me—too much new, too soon. I close my eyes and try to think of one thing that is constant in my life. But all I see is my mother's face, and the fact of her death.

14. Can a lifetime of searching bring us closer to the truth?

THREE

BREAK ON THROUGH

OCTOBER 20TH. It's fifteen days till my first exam, seven weeks since Mom died. Each date is a marker. One step closer equals one step away.

Taryn.

Party, Friday night, a friend's house. Wanna come?

♥ Will

Sure. Will I know anyone?

T ♥

You know me.

I have no clean boxers. My T-shirt has a hole under the arm. The jeans I am wearing could walk out the front door on their own. Nobody knows the whereabouts of my socks. Adam lends me a pair. I am wearing corporate socks to a party. The world has gone into a slow decline.

Taryn has on a backless red dress. Her hair is touching her spine. So beautiful. I open the door for her and scramble in behind her onto the backseat.

"Hey, I'm not your bloody chauffeur," says Adam, pouting. "Hi, Taryn."

She smiles. I look at Adam as I jump on her, cradle her head against the car door.

"And no sex while I'm driving, it puts me off."

I kiss her, kiss her hard, before we sit up and put on our seat belts.

"So, where is this party anyway?" he asks, pulling out of her driveway.

"Up on Elders Street. Number 27. And you're not staying."

"Now why would I want to hang around with a bunch of juveniles?" He looks at us in the rearview mirror. "My apologies, Taryn. I was talking about his friends."

"Doesn't sound good," she says, laughing. "And here I was looking forward to meeting them."

"That's if I still have any after I walk in there wearing pinstriped socks."

"Hey, I bought those in Singapore, they're good socks. So, no vomit on them, all right?"

"Speaking of which, can you swing past the liquor store?" About time I started acting my age.

Parties give me stage fright but, as Taryn steps out of the car ahead of me, I get a red carpet feeling.

"I don't know anybody," she says, eyeing the people standing on the lawn. I slip my arm around her. In my other hand I have a bottle of vodka in a brown paper bag. Kids from school nod at me, their eyes on her. On that ruby dress.

"Hey, Will. Who's this?" A girl from my Lit class has her hand on my shoulder. "Hi, I'm Emma."

"This is Taryn. Is Seb here?"

"Yeah, he's in the kitchen. Eating, of course," says Emma.

Taryn smiles at Emma as we go into the house. "Is she your ex?"

"Christ, no." I laugh. "She hardly ever speaks to me."

"Could've fooled me." She presses me against the hallway wall. Her dress is paper-thin.

"You shouldn't wear things like this in public."

"Why?"

"Because it's hard walking around with one of these. I feel like a dog in heat."

I draw her hand down to my jeans. She laughs. "Come on, introduce me to Seb."

In the kitchen, Seb's wrapped around a bowl of chips, his voice struggling above the music. "Good to see you, Will."

I remember the last time we spoke, my inglorious escape.

He wipes a hand on his jeans and offers it to Taryn. "Hi, I'm Seb."

"What's with the handshaking?" I ask, leaning against the counter.

Taryn nudges me. "Hi, Seb. Finally, we meet."

A shout invades from the next room.

"What's going on in there?"

"Oh, that's Ritchie," says Seb, checking out Taryn now that

she's distracted. "He took something before everybody got here, and he keeps shouting *I am the Lizard King.*"

Ritchie comes writhing through the door, feral hair, sweat oozing from his face. His bare chest has a diagonal scratch across it, and his fly's undone.

"Break on through, break on through," he chants, grabbing himself a beer out of a tub of ice.

"Thinks he's Jim Morrison. Loser."

"Who? Morrison?" asks Taryn.

"No, Ritchie," laughs Seb.

"My dad's a big Doors fan," says Taryn. "Hey, Will, what about a drink?"

"Mine too," nods Seb.

"My dad's more your elevator music kind of guy," I say, holding up the vodka. "You want some, Seb?"

"No, I'm all right." He points to an almost full bottle of beer on the bench. "Slow drinker."

I fill two glasses half with vodka, half with some cranberry juice I find on the counter, and hand one to Taryn. She takes a sip and coughs. "You trying to get me drunk?"

"Well, I was wondering what you're like once you've got a few drinks in you. Bet there's a spare room upstairs."

Seb returns to his bowl of chips.

"Slut," she says, kissing me on the neck, the vodka already seeping into me, the music getting that slick kind of flow, the red of her dress like a lure. My hand . . .

"I am the Lizard King!!!"

"Always thought there was something reptilian about Ritchie," says Seb, shoving in a handful of chips. Ritchie, jerking in time with the music, makes another tour of the room.

* * *

Red angel, that's what she is, her thigh created for my hand. She brings me a message, her eyelashes feathers. The message is one of love. Of skin. Of reaching out and touching something else. She is an idea, hovering above me, that beyond all this, she is what I make of her. That I am not what I am, but what I choose to be, what my mind, my heart, requires me to become.

Corporate socks are resistant to vomit.

Vodka doesn't smell.

But pizza does.

"Jesus, it's lucky it's me picking you up and not Dad," grunts Adam as he drags my legs into the car. "Did he polish off the whole bottle on his own?"

"I gave him a bit of a hand," says Taryn. "And so did the Lizard King."

"What?"

"Don't ask," she says, flopping down next to me.

"Idiot." Adam shoves my feet in and slams the door.

I can feel a dark pulse. It's starting in my chest, working up a vein in my throat into my head. It's the pump of blood, a metallic taste on my tongue. The dilation of nostrils. The forming of fists. As the car starts up, I lean fiercely into the corner of the seat.

"You okay, Will? Hey, Adam, maybe you'd better stop. I think he's going to throw up."

"Don't you dare throw up in Dad's car."

The door opens.

My head drops back. Smashes into something that doesn't give.

Adam's pulling me out, hauling me by the chest, his fingers

digging into my ribs. Hurting me. I spin around and hit him, hard in the mouth.

"What the . . . ?"

"Will!"

I go for him, throw him to the ground, my body steel, all my angles thrust into him. There's screaming, something clutching at my leg, a ruby dress. Red car. A blow to the stomach, my guts emptying violently all over grass.

Slumped.

Adam is sitting on his ass, wiping his mouth. "You are one mean bastard when you're drunk."

Taryn glares at me, hands on her hips. The world is already hammering into a small ugly ball at the base of my neck. At both temples.

I am what I am, and nothing more.

The next morning, there is no next morning, there's only an afternoon. A pounding on my door. "Will, I hope you're studying."

"Been working on my math, Dad, I'll be out in a minute."

I drop out of bed, smelling of disgust. My body has mutinied, left me on a small raft without water. I have a salt-dried tongue. Well, pickled actually. The vision of a clear empty bottle, red label, liquid pain. I crawl to the bathroom and do my best, then on to the kitchen.

"You look almost as bad as your brother. Said he got into a fight in a pub last night. Can you imagine? Adam in a fight."

"Where is he?"

"Out. Had somebody he had to meet."

I get myself a glass of orange juice. The thought of cereal . . .

"Oh, and Taryn rang. I called you but you must have been asleep. Wanted to know if you were going over this afternoon. I said it would depend on how your study was going."

"Got it all covered, Dad. Have I ever failed anything?"

"Well, no, but you seem . . . changed."

It's a good time to talk but my head won't allow it, and the orange juice is having an argument with my stomach about whether it should stay. "The only constant is change," I say, like a hungover incarnation of Samara.

"Did you learn that for your English exam?"

"Yeah, Dad. See, nothing to worry about."

"Good, good," he says, taking a swig from a bottle of beer.

"Since when did you start drinking on Saturday afternoons? If Mom were here . . ." I want to keep going but my stomach says no.

"If your mom were here she'd say, *Bit early, Michael.*"

I hear her voice in his. Dad pats me on the shoulder, pauses, pats me again. "You're a lot like her."

He's waiting, like a kid at an ice cream counter, and I want to say, *Except I'm here, Dad,* but I can't. First, because my head feels ready to collapse on itself. Second, this is not the way we do things. With us, truth has to fall through the gaps.

"Better not keep Taryn waiting," I say, staggering every movement so I don't lose the juice. "You know how women are."

"Yeah. You all right to get yourself over there?"

"Sure, Dad."

"Then I think I'll get myself another beer."

When I get to Taryn's, Ray and Sandy are watching some show about art. No sports in this house. Taryn pilots me into the kitchen, pours a glass of water and drops something in. She hasn't kissed me yet.

"Here, drink this. Gastrolyte. It'll rehydrate that brain of yours. Tastes like sweet aspirin, but as long as you don't chuck it up you'll be right."

I do as I'm told. It's fizzy and foul, but a small price to pay.

"So, how was Adam this morning?"

"Don't know. He was gone by the time I got up. Was it awful?"

"Yes. What happened? Are you usually like that when you're drunk?"

"God, no." I reach for her hand, but she's removed from it. It's just flesh.

"Well, how am I supposed to know? I didn't recognize you last night."

She's thinking, she hardly knows me; she's thinking, she's made a mistake. "Things have been a bit messed up lately," I say.

She frowns.

"No, I don't mean us."

"Why did you hit him? Do you know that much?"

"Not sure. I haven't hit him for ages, not since we were really little, and that was mostly defending myself. Maybe it's got something to do with how he's been since Mom died. I thought he'd be more supportive but he's been a real prick."

Her hand has life in it again. She reaches over and touches my face, strokes my cheek with the back of her hand. God, she's so gentle, the perfect antidote to life. "You should talk to him about it."

"Yeah, maybe I will."

"So, do you think that head of yours can handle a little

music? Samara and I have been sorting out our favorite music; we're going to make a CD."

"Sure."

Taryn leads me to Samara's room. She's sitting cross-legged on the floor next to her stereo—I remember the last time I saw her like that, but that's as far as it goes.

"Heard you went on a bit of a bender last night."

"Yeah, and paying for it."

Samara laughs. "Karmic, definitely karmic."

"What are you listening to?"

"Nusrat Fateh Ali Khan."

"Who?"

The flash from the flint of the lighter annoys my brain as Samara lights some more incense, the wailing of the music only making it worse. "Nusrat Fateh Ali Khan. He's a qawwali singer."

"Well, that explains everything."

"Sufi music." She looks at me with a grin. "The mystics of Islam."

This is all doing my head in—the part that's still alive. "Yeah, I know what a sufi is," I say, even though I don't.

Taryn: "Jeff Buckley was into Nusrat Fateh Ali Khan."

"Is that what got you into, what's it called?"

"Qawwali? No." Samara hands me the CD cover. It's got writing I don't recognize and it looks pirated. "Actually, I first heard it when I was in Pakistan, hanging out with these drug lords. Don't ask."

As if I was going to. Samara stretches on her back, her hair fanning around her, probably dreaming of tall, dark guys doing coke. I recognize the incense, forget its name. Taryn lays her head against mine. The music stretches around us, sounding of deserts, of birds soaring above sand—the lonely search for something real on a Saturday afternoon.

Memory.

A Saturday in June. Dad and Adam have gone to a football match but I didn't want to go because Adam's team is in first place. I hear music filtering from the living room—Mom's sprawled on the couch, her arms stretched above her head. *"Oh, hold me like a baby."* I watch her without moving, mesmerized. "I thought you were reading in your bedroom. It's Suzanne Vega," she offers over the music as she straightens her shirt.

Apart from Pop's funeral, that's the only time I heard my mother sing.

LIFE'S LONGING

SUNDAY MORNING, Adam wakes me, a red bruise trailing the bone of his left cheek. "So, what happened, Will?"

"I don't know, I just lost it. You okay?"

"What's going on? Is it exams, or is this about Mom?"

"You really want to know?"

"Asked, didn't I?"

So, I tell him, everything, from the wake with the sinister great aunts, right up to the party at Ritchie's, and he listens, doesn't say a word. Doesn't even nod.

"That's quite a story," says Adam, once I've finished. I wait for him to comment, to offer some kind of judgment on the saga of my grief. He shifts at the end of my bed. "I've been thinking."

"Yeah?"

"About why I stayed?"

"Okay." I can tell he wants me to haul it out of him but I reckon it's time he did that himself.

"It's got something to do with what Mom said the last time I saw her."

"Uh-huh."

Adam taps his fist gently into his hand. His bruise is almost flattering on his cheek. "She said that, with me gone all the time, it felt like we were no longer a family. That something was coming undone."

"She always was good at explaining that kind of thing."

"Yeah, she was."

He sits unmoving on the end of the bed, and I know the longer the silence, the less likely he is to speak. "Adam . . ."

"Listen, you going to the christening today?"

"What christening?"

"Our new cousin. Rachel's baby son. Didn't Dad tell you?"

"Nah. Nobody tells me anything."

"I've got a couple of spare shirts. You could borrow one if you want." Adam looks at *The Tibetan Book of Living and Dying* on the stack by my bed. "So, do you reckon you're getting close?"

"To what?"

"To finding an answer."

"Not sure there is one," I say picking up the book. The gold lettering of the title is hard to decipher in the light sifting through the curtains.

"Do you think I could borrow it?"

"Go for it."

He flicks through the first few pages. "*Impermanence*, huh?"

I shake my head as he shoves the book under his arm and leaves, absently stroking the bruise on his cheek.

Aunty Rachel is hyper when we get there, scuttling around making sure everyone knows everyone else. Turns out it's not technically a christening—it's called a naming day instead. The baby's almost three months old. My cousin was born exactly one month before my mother died. His life will always be a calculation of that.

"Your mom and I were raised Catholics, but we both gave that up a long time ago," whispers Aunty Rachel to Adam and me. When she says *mom* her face goes rigid and the baby starts to cry. It's kind of ugly as far as babies go, basically a collection of pink rolls of fat. And it's very loud.

"Was I like that?" I ask Adam.

"Not unless I pinched you."

"Bastard."

"As far as I remember you were a pretty quiet baby and you weren't that ugly."

"Sssshhh."

Aunty Rachel herds everyone into the back garden to a wooden arch shrouded in roses. I remember Mom always loved it, wanted Dad to build one at our place, but he never did. "Welcome, everybody, to Sam's naming day," she begins.

She looks proudly at Uncle Derek who's trying to smile above Sam's squawks. He gets to hold the baby. Uncle Carl and his wife, Catriona, are there with their three little kids; all my cousins are younger than me. There are heaps of people I don't know, which reminds me of the wake. Thankfully, no great-aunts. And there's Dad, gawking at that archway, not listening at all.

Aunty Rachel squints at Sam's din. "The following is a passage from Kahlil Gibran."

> *Your children are not your children.*
> *They are the sons and daughters of Life's longing for itself.*

Dad turns to Adam and me, a triangle of glances that we hold as my aunt reads poetry and my cousin wails.

After the ceremony, everybody goes inside to have something to eat.

"You coming?" asks Adam. He looks good in his suit.

"No. I think I'll stick around outside for a bit. Don't think I can handle Aunty Rachel."

"Sure, I'll bring you back something to eat if you like."

"Thanks."

A couple of my little cousins are kicking a soccer ball around the backyard and it's getting a bit rough. One of them, Essie, comes over to me—I think she's about four. "What's your name?" she asks, rocking on her shoes.

"Will. I'm your cousin, remember?"

"Maybe. What are you playing?"

"I was thinking."

"Why?"

I smile. "Adults like to think about things."

"Are you an adult?"

"Sort of."

"What are you thinking?"

I look over at the rose arch. "I was wondering what it would be like if my mom was here."

"Where is she?"

What do you say to a kid? Essie's staring at me, waiting for an answer. "She's dead."

"Is she in heaven?"

"I don't know. What do you think?"

"Maybe she's in that rose. The white one." She points to the archway.

"Oh, yeah. Why's that?"

"My mommy is beautiful like a rose." She grabs my hand and leads me over to the roses. "Can you pick one? The pointy bits hurt my fingers."

"You mean the thorns."

She nods and points to one that's still opening. "That one, please."

I bend it at a joint but it doesn't come easily. I go carefully so as not to bruise the petals and finally it breaks off. Its center has a tinge of pink.

"Here you go."

"She's in there," says Essie, lifting the rose to me.

"Who?"

"Your mommy. Look."

So I look, the scent of the rose rising to my face like sweet wet grass. There's a beetle crawling among the petals; it keeps slipping. "There's a bug in there," I say.

Essie nods and waits, and I allow myself to slip into her logic, a mother, a flower. If she stood under this rosebush long enough maybe they share something on a molecular level, some of her memory is held in its water. But I know that's not what Essie means.

"So, you think my mom is in this rose."

"Yes."

"So do I," I say.

Essie strokes the rose, careful not to crush it. "You can keep it, I have a mommy." She lets it drop into my hand, and runs off to join her two brothers who are wrestling over the soccer ball on the grass.

Adam comes over carrying a napkin and a plate piled with food. “Getting a bit claustrophobic in there. Rachel was talking about Mom and started to cry so I left her with Dad. Probably do them both good.”

I take a bite of a chocolate éclair.

Adam frowns. “Oi, you’re meant to eat your veggies first.”

“I’ve been having an interesting conversation with Essie. She reckons Mom’s in that rose.”

“Kids, huh?”

Adam picks up the rose, holds it to his face, a petal brushing his bruise. He breathes in deeply, turns to me. “Come on, eat up. We should be getting home.”

Essie’s last comment to me as she left with her brothers: “We don’t know when we will die, but our bodies do.”

DERVISH

THEY SAY IF YOU HEAR about the same thing three times in a row, you should take note. Mystics. That's the word I seem to be hearing right now. I found this site about whirling meditation, guys spinning around and around. Faster and faster they go, arms wide, long hats pointing to the sky, sometimes for an hour, till, through loss of ego, they reach the *perfect*. No sitting in mountain caves, they just twirl, mystical white spinning tops, and when they return from wherever it is they go, they press their belly buttons to the earth, and are ready to love, to serve. Dervishes, they're called, a kind of Sufi. What some people won't do to get closer to the truth. And me, what do I do? Read a few books from the library, surf on the Net. Where's the passion in that? I feel itchy, on the inside. I need action. To whirl myself into a frenzy. To *feel* what it means to be alive.

In my notebook, I copy a quote from Rumi, founder of the Whirling Dervishes:

If your knowledge of fire has been turned to certainty by words alone, then seek to be cooked by the fire itself. Don't abide in borrowed certainty. There is no real certainty until you burn; if you wish for this, sit down in the fire.

Take the day off from school with me tomorrow. There's something I want to do.

♥ Will

Such as? I don't want to sound like your dad, but do you think it's a good idea with your exams coming soon? Besides, I've never skipped class.

T ♥

Good time to start. Anyone home at your place tomorrow?

Yeah, Dad. He's working on an article all day, he said. I don't know. I don't think it's a good idea. Come around after school.

T ♥

Will? You still there?

The girl at the checkout looks younger than me and for an instant I get this premonition of what life might be like if I fail my exams, if I don't do what everybody says I should. To hell with it, I could be dead tomorrow. I need to treat life like those Buddhist monks I read about who turned their teacups over every night before they went to bed and let their fires go out because they knew there was no guarantee they'd ever wake up.

"That'll be $9.80," says the girl, shoving the spray can into a bag.

I give her a ten-dollar note. "Keep the change."

"I can't. Here, take it and stick it in the charity box over there." She points to a plastic dog with a slot in its head. "Better than giving it to these guys. Bloody corporate robbers."

It's then that I notice the girl's name is Cherry and her fingernails are painted black.

"What are you going to do with that?" She grins, nodding at my plastic bag.

"Nothing."

"Yeah, right." She leans over the counter and whispers, "I'm getting off in half an hour. Will you wait for me?"

First thought, Taryn, followed by, maybe it's time for a little fire. "Sure, why not? I'll meet you at the café downstairs, the one next to the sushi bar. By the way, my name's Will."

"Where there's a will." She laughs, too loud for the lady behind me. "Won't be long. Only a few more people to rob."

The coffee's bitter and I'm thinking this was a dumb idea. Somebody I know might see me. Tell Taryn. Tell Dad. And what's with the anarchist checkout chick?

"So, Will, what's your tag?" Cherry arrives wearing a bright red top in keeping with the theme.

"Don't have one."

"Well, have you at least picked a spot?"

"There's this place I've seen from the train, under a bridge. It's about three stations down."

"Cool. So, only the one color then."

I drink the last bad mouthful of coffee. "I'll only be writing words."

"Sounds like you've got a plan. Come on, let's get out of here."

It's cooler under the bridge and our mission feels nobler away from people's eyes. I know everything about Cherry—how many half siblings she has, that her father's gay, the name of the first guy she ever slept with, and how useless he was. How the second one was *fucking great!* She looks like she'll jump me if she gets the chance even though she's only half my size—her fierceness makes me feel like a dumb kid and an old man all at once.

"I can't believe you've never done ecstasy. Until you've dropped an E you haven't lived." In Cherry's world, there is a long list of things you must do in order to have lived. I'm about to do one of them. "So, what are you going to write?"

"All of us are creatures of a day."

"Why?"

"Because I think it's true."

"Fair enough. Did you make it up?"

"No, Marcus Aurelius did."

"Who's Marcus Aurelius?"

"I can't believe you haven't read Marcus Aurelius. Until you've read his *Meditations*, you haven't lived."

"Loser." She shoves me hard, then steadies me, hands on my arms. "Train coming. Move back."

"Move back? Shouldn't we get out from under the bridge?"

"No fun," she says pressing her back into the wall. I do the same, the mortar jagged against my hands. The roar of the train entering the tunnel, getting louder, the warning rush of wind, and suddenly it's there, the sound of metal on metal, a violent pitch. The flash of silver. I stop breathing. Cherry screams. So loud, so loud, then gone, the tail end of it speeding down the track.

"You okay?"

"Sure," says Cherry, her hair blown off her face. "I always scream with stuff like that. Gets your heart going. Come on, we'd better hurry, in case the driver saw us and phones it in."

I pull the spray can out of my bag and test it on the wall. The paint spits. Cherry laughs. "You have to shake it first, you idiot."

"I know that."

Overhead, cars judder across the bridge. There's a long patch of black where somebody's painted over some graffiti, so I start spraying on that.

"White on black. Very good. Easy to see." Cherry straddles a track to watch me as I work. Her boots crunch on the gravel and smoke from her cigarette curls around her shoulder—now that the train's gone there's no wind. I spray into grooves and over bumps. I have to keep standing back to make sure the whole thing is straight. The sentence seems longer now that every letter requires effort. Both of us, me and Marcus Aurelius, are earning our place on the wall.

"Your first masterpiece," says Cherry when I finish. "Better get out of here now, just in case."

She grinds the butt into the polished track with her boot while I wipe the paint that has dripped down my fingers onto the wall. Hope they can't take prints from this. I shove the can back into its plastic bag—I'll dump it at the station, or maybe I'll keep it and write something somewhere else. Cover the whole city in philosophical graffiti. I need to get myself a tag.

On the way back on the train, we pass under the bridge. Two cops are standing next to our words. Cherry waves at them as we go past. "At least they've learned something today," she laughs, kissing me on the cheek. "Can we do this again?"

"I've got a girlfriend."

"I didn't ask you to have sex with me," she says, grinning. She pulls out a pen and writes on my hand. "That's my number. Call me. Whatever. I'm getting off here."

"Thanks," I say.

"Thanks, yourself." Her bright red top is a beacon moving along the platform. I pull out my notebook.

> *15. Will others get burned if I sit down in the fire?*

Memory.

Mom's gone. Dad said she went to visit an old friend, but she didn't tell me—Mom always tells me if she's going away. It's not so bad because we get to eat takeout all week and stay up late. I've just turned six. Dad forgets to tell us to go to bed. He forgets to take out the garbage and the bin starts to stink.

When she comes back she's wearing a new red dress. For a few days she keeps trying to hug me whenever I walk into the room. She leaves her packed bag sitting by her bed for ages, until one day it's gone. I find the red dress in her wardrobe, scrunched up and shoved to the back.

* * *

Wednesday night. Supermarket parking lot wall.

To live each day as though one's last.

—Marcus Aurelius

Thursday, 3 a.m. Side of the school gym. With Cherry.

A man who has learned how to die has unlearned how to be a slave.

—Montaigne

Friday after school. Other side of the railway bridge. Cherry couldn't make it, she had to work, but that's okay, this one I want to do on my own.

I get the can out of my bag and give it a good shake. The Marcus Aurelius quote I did last time is still there, nobody's painted over it yet—I'll have to do the letters smaller because there's less room on this side. Too many tags.

I pull my notebook out of my bag and open it to the new quote, write *You must have*, and get halfway through *chaos*, when I hear it—the screech, the oscillating rattle, the fading of all other sound. Spray can secure against the wall, I go to climb out of the tunnel but my foot freezes on a rock at the bottom of the bank. I go back inside, to the middle of the tunnel, to its stretched light, press my shoulder blades against the wall.

And then it comes, hurtling metal, the wind, the roar, a mix of suction and repulsion, the blur of faces and glass. The void. My hands against the bricks, shoulders reaching forward, my foot lifting. My heart rallies to the rhythm of the wheels, clack, clack, clack. My eyes closed, I step away from the wall, feel the reflection of metal on my face and I fall forward, falling, falling . . .

Plummet into space, Nietzsche's words in my head.

You must have chaos within you to give birth to a dancing star.

"And I thought you were taking me somewhere romantic," says Taryn. We are in the Safeway parking lot.

"Oh, but it is, sort of. You'll see."

A woman wheeling a shopping cart back to her car gives us a "loitering teenagers" kind of look. I smile back.

"Ta-da." We're standing in front of Marcus Aurelius—*To live each day as though one's last.*

"Did you do that?"

I nod and hug her. "What do you think?"

"About what you wrote, or the fact that you've taken up vandalism as your new thing?"

I let her go. "Either."

"Don't look at me like that, Will. All I was thinking . . ."

"What?"

"Well, is this really the right thing to be doing?"

I fling my arms out toward the shoppers, their shopping carts loaded on a Saturday night. "Look at these people. They're surrounded by stuff, but there's no real thought."

"People have to eat, Will. Anyway, I'm sure, if you asked, they'd have their own philosophy on life."

"You reckon?"

I kick an empty cigarette pack but it doesn't lift; it crushes under my feet instead. Taryn's finger fumbles the end of my sleeve. "Will, I don't want to sound cruel, but I think what happened to you has kind of warped your whole view of things, at least for the moment. In time . . ."

"In time I'll learn to shut my eyes like the rest of the world."

"Can we go somewhere else?"

"I think not."

I stare past her at a piece of gum smudged into the asphalt and I lean against the wall, next to the word *last*. "Anyway, I'm meeting someone later."

"Who?"

"Nobody you know."

"This is *so* wrong, Will. Look at me."

I stare into those eyes.

"We love each other, remember?"

I nod. She puts her arms around me and my hand settles in the sway of her back. "Let's go home, Will."

"Sure."

"And that person you had to meet?"

"It can wait."

Her mouth fumbles its way to mine. Her kiss is wary at first, then fierce.

Samara's getting friendly with a bottle of Cointreau when we arrive at the house. She pours some for us. "Cheers."

It tastes like oranges and it has a kick. Taryn bangs her emptied glass on the table. "Shut up and keep serving. Whose is it anyway?"

"Mine. Got it duty-free on my way back."

"It's delicious," says Taryn. "So, tell us about those drug lords you were hanging around with in Pakistan. What kind of stuff were they selling?"

Samara looks sideways at Taryn as she refills her glass. "Mostly heroin and opium. It comes from Afghanistan over the Khyber Pass."

"What were drug dealers doing listening to Sufi music?" I ask.

"Everybody listens to qawwali over there. Don't get me wrong, they were probably quite spiritual."

Taryn. "Yeah, in a drug-induced kind of way."

I turn to Samara. "So, do Sufis do drugs?"

"Don't know, never met any. But I know sadhus do."

Seems I get one word worked out and another shows up. "What's a sadhu?"

Taryn bangs her glass on the table again, next to the groove that she cut, and refills her glass herself. Samara smiles. "A sadhu is a holy man. They're all over India, mostly Hindus. They give up everything and go on the road. In some states, government shops sell hash and opium to sadhus for religious purposes." She raises her eyebrows. "Or, at least, that's what I heard."

"Really? So, what's hash meant to do?" I ask Samara as Taryn throws her head back and drains her glass.

"Free your mind. Help you get in contact with Shiva, Consciousness, whatever you want to call it."

"Have you ever tried?"

"What? Hash? Sure, but not for that reason, just to get high. I can roll us a joint if you like," offers Samara. "I've got some in my room."

"What about your parents?"

"They're out. Anyway, I wouldn't worry about them, they went to university in the seventies. Still, better come into my room, don't want to stink up the whole house."

Taryn jabs me with her elbow. "You've never smoked weed, have you?"

"Never got around to it," I mutter.

Taryn puts some music on while Samara gets a plastic bag out of the drawer by her bed. She lights a joint, takes a deep puff, and hands it to Taryn. Fugitive smoke curls from her nose.

"Man, that's strong," murmurs Taryn, sucking in her breath. The end is moist, the smoke harsh as it enters my throat, and it's hard to resist the urge to cough. I feel dizzy but not much else. I hand it back to Samara and it continues like this, the music and the joint going around.

"Let's go," says Taryn, tugging on my arm. It's going to come out of my shoulder if she doesn't stop. I try to stand but my legs wilt. "Will."

"You're all right. Off you go, just don't make too much noise though." Samara's lying on her back, finishing off the joint.

I manage to get up and stay up. Taryn drags me to her room, lowers me onto the bed, starts winding my T-shirt off, but I don't want to be undressed. I want to sit in a corner, not close my eyes—tried that already, not good—maybe look at the wall.

"Taryn. I'm . . . sorry."

Her hand reaches into my jeans but only the rims of my eyelids feel hard. She presses herself against me, legs tangled, but it's like being caged. I need to push her away. "Taryn . . ."

"What the hell is up with you, Will?"

"Nothing."

She climbs on top of me and pins me down, her marmalade hair flaming around her face. "Who were you going to meet?"

"Nobody."

"Don't lie."

"Just this girl. She's been helping with the graffiti."

"Great." Taryn covers her face with her hands. "This is all falling apart, Will."

"No, it's not. Don't, Taryn. You're stoned, that's all." She feels far away, looming, must be the dope.

"Obviously not stoned enough." She rolls off and turns away from me. "Why don't you go home."

I wait, time stretching out in incalculable units, but her back blocks me, so I get up and leave.

Outside, on their driveway, I look up to make sure of the stars, but clouds have laid siege to the sky and absconded with the moon.

It's a long way home. My feet are colossal, unfamiliar. Traitors they seem to me, especially when I need them most. There's a brick wall with jagged mortar like the tunnel where I almost stepped under the train. My knuckles snag on its roughness as I pass. I let my hand trail behind me and the skin shreds, bump, bump, bump against the cement. The pain is softened by the dope. I think of the church and the candles, the seductive burn of the flame, the moment that was too much. But this is different, messier, and I know there's blood.

I look at my hand. The skin is torn on two of the knuckles. All of the fingers are bleeding except for the thumb. I shudder, even though it doesn't really hurt, and laugh. It's my left hand, not the one I use to write—that's me, always cautious even in destruction, allowing some way back.

The sky is hovering, the streets still barren, the only life a black cat, tail wound around a tree like a prophecy, and me with a hollowness in my guts. Nothing mystical, just wanting to leave myself behind. And what will save me—love, philosophy, some higher force?

I keep moving, leave the wall behind, the one with a trail of me stuck to it, little bits of Will. Up ahead is Degrazis', I'm almost home, and there's the church. Above its sign there's a light, and they've changed the quote—it says, *Come to Him in love.* I take out my keys, lean against the glass that protects the words, and scratch, *God is dead.* A smear of blood soaks into the word *God* like a tattoo.

Life according to Nietzsche.

> *God is dead. God remains dead. And we have killed him. How shall we, murderers of all murderers, console ourselves? That which was the holiest and mightiest of all that the world has yet possessed has bled to death under our knives. Who will wipe this blood off us? . . . Is not the greatness of this deed too great for us?*

And here's the mother of all questions:

> *Must we not ourselves become gods simply to be worthy of it?*

GLIMPSES FROM THE CAVERN

IT'S SUNDAY AFTERNOON and I'm having an *existential crisis.* On the bus on the way to Seb's, that's what the woman said after she leaned over and asked me what was wrong. When she told me I looked like "death warmed over," I answered, "We're all lukewarm things waiting to die." But she didn't turn away, like she was meant to. She nodded and whispered, "Existential crisis."

What the hell's that, I thought, but it turned out she was a mind reader too. She spent the next five minutes explaining. Basic summary below.

I am reacting to my mother's death and to my sudden realization of my own mortality by going into a psychological head spin because I have realized that life has no predestined meaning. I must either find comfort in some form of religion or seek my own meaning to existence, and embrace the freedom that comes with it, as well as the responsibility. For further information see Jean-Paul Sartre, famous French existentialist.

"This is my stop," she said, and got off the bus. She was gone when I looked out the window, making me wonder whether she was ever there at all.

* * *

I throw myself down on Seb's bed.

"You haven't come to study, have you?" he asks, looking up from his books.

"Nobody was home."

"So?"

"I didn't feel like being alone."

"Okay, but keep quiet. I'm working on those math problems Radcliffe gave us to practice on and nothing's going in."

"Do you need a hand?"

"No, I have to work them out for myself. We're not all smart pricks like you."

"I'll be good, I promise. Not a word."

Existential crisis—sounds better than losing it. Wonder what Taryn's doing, apart from hating my guts? I'd hate me, too. I should call her, but right now I feel too sick of myself. Though, there is also this part of me that needs to do justice to my grief.

"Seb?"

"Yes, Will." There's menace in his voice.

"Do you ever worry about there being no meaning to your life? That it's all utterly random?"

"Now, you see, that's what I like about you, Will. I ask you not to interrupt me and, instead of asking what there is to eat, you want me to analyze my own existence."

"Sorry."

"No, no, that's fine. Seriously. I mean the exam's only a week away and I'm having absolutely no trouble focusing on one of the most important days of my life." He taps his pen on the desk. "Listen, go talk to Dad. He loves that shit."

"Okay," I say, rolling off the bed. "And, hey, if you need help, I did those during class already and they aren't that bad."

"Get lost, genius, before I perform a live vivisection on you with this." He waves his compass at me as I go.

Seb's dad is in the living room squatting over a box of records, his jeans drooping down around his ass. His old Stones T-shirt has a hole above the word *tour*. "Hi, Daniel."

"Will. Haven't seen you around much lately. Been studying?"

"Yeah, sort of. What are you doing?"

"Sorting my record collection. Bit obsessive about it and, as the wife's not home, thought I'd indulge."

"Seb was saying you're into the Doors."

"Would've died for them when I was a kid."

"Yeah, really. So tell me about the Lizard King?"

"Morrison? Mad bastard, he was. Bit of a visionary, I guess you'd say."

"Oh, yeah, kind of like a guru?"

"Kind of like a junkie, that's what. They were into peyote, among other things," he says, his fingers plowing rows in his stubby gray hair.

"Peyote?"

"Cactus juice. It's a hallucinogenic. The American Indians use it for ceremonies. That's how Morrison worked out the lizard was his totem animal. Or so he said." Daniel pulls out a record with a huge open mouth on the cover, a scared pink face. "Some people saw him as a shaman, thought he could create a kind of link between this world and the next."

"What do you reckon?"

"Reckon if you take enough drugs you'll believe anything," he says, sliding the record back in.

"Have you ever taken peyote?"

"No, but I took acid a few times when I was younger. Sort of does the same thing. Not sure your dad would like me telling you this stuff. It's about now I'm meant to give you the talk about how drugs fry your brain."

"Consider yourself off the hook," I say, sinking into the couch.

"They got their name from this book called *The Doors of Perception*. It was about a guy who took peyote. The title came from a poem by Blake. Have you heard of him?"

"Sure. Not as stupid as I look."

"Nothing stupid about you, Will. Never was." Daniel sits on the floor but can't quite manage to cross his legs. "You're a good kid and I think it's awful what happened to your mom."

We both study the carpet. "Thanks, Daniel."

"Any time, any time."

"So can you get peyote here?"

"I don't know, but it's serious stuff, especially if you're already feeling a bit, you know." Daniel's eyes fall on the cuts on my hand, my knuckles an uneven line of Band-Aids.

"I was just interested."

"I can put the Doors on if you like, or have you got studying to do?"

"Nah, I'm taking a break."

A smile comes over his face. "*Strange Days*, 1967 release, original condition. Only these fingers touch them," he says, wiggling them in front of me. He puts the record on the turntable. "I trust you've seen one of these."

"Sure."

"This is one of my favorites. 'Moonlight Drive.' "

He lowers the needle. There's a crackle as the music begins, a bluesy keyboard, eerie slide guitar. Daniel closes his eyes and lets his head drop back, and there he is, the Lizard King, his voice trippy, earnest, riding the music that sounds like the theme to *Sesame Street*, as he sings about surrendering to worlds that wait and swimming to the moon.

Back home, I look through my collection of Blake's poems till I find these words from *The Marriage of Heaven and Hell*:

> *If the doors of perception were cleansed everything would appear to man as it is, infinite.*
>
> *For man has closed himself up, till he sees all things through narrow chinks of his cavern.*

The raggedy edge. There's only one person I know who can take me there.

The gutters are all cobblestones, the houses thin slices, the only gardens a few dried-up plants in pots. The house she takes me to has an old armchair out in front with stuffing sprouting from the seams like tufts of grass. She opens the rusty gate—I could step over it but she's tiny, with her black hair all feathery, none of it the same length.

"My brother's name's Dave, but everybody calls him Hummer," says Cherry, as she knocks on the door. "It's his avatar. He's seriously into gaming."

After a minute, there's movement inside, the sound of locks being undone. A short, pale guy opens the door, his eyes squinting at the light. "Hey," says Hummer, and skulks back into the house, his long jeans swishing on the carpet.

"That's about as sociable as he gets," says Cherry, taking my hand and leading me in. The hall is cluttered and dark and at the end of it there's a lounge room lit only by a TV. A band's playing on it that I don't know.

"Sit down," he says, leaving the room.

The couch sinks low and Cherry and I almost fall on top of each other, her thigh half the length of mine.

"Hummer says it's good stuff."

"Great," I say, as if I have an idea what good is.

"What happened to your hand?"

"Nothing."

She raises her thin eyebrows at me as Hummer comes back with a piece of foil in his hand. Inside, two sugar cubes. Cherry takes one, "Here goes," and drops it into her mouth. She hands me the other and it's cold on my tongue at first before it begins to dissolve. "Suck it," she says. "It'll take a while to kick in."

Hummer: "I'll be in my room. Drinks are in the fridge."

"Thanks," I say, but he just raises an eyebrow and disappears into the hall. "You guys don't look much alike."

"Different fathers. His dad's a complete shit."

"And yours?"

"He's all right. Don't see him much. He works in big mines, makes heaps of cash. Takes me out to these fancy restaurants whenever he's in town. That's his thing. Mom hates his guts but he's okay."

"What's your mom like?"

"Fat. What about you? What's your mom like?"

"Dead."

"Shit. When?"

"About two months ago."

"Why didn't you say?"

"I guess it's nice being with someone who doesn't have it in the back of their mind every time they look at me."

"Did it fuck you up? I mean, my mother's a fat tart but it'd mess me up if she died."

"Depends how you define *fucked up*. I mean, it's Tuesday morning, my exams start in three days, and I've just taken acid for the first time. Some people might call that *fucked up*."

"Where I come from that's pretty bloody normal. Is that why you're doing this? Because of your mom?"

I stare up at the ceiling. There's a watermark in the plaster, its brown edges forming a butterfly.

"You don't have to tell me if you don't want to," she whispers, looking up at the stain.

"I've been reading about peyote."

"Is that another philosopher?"

"Nah, it's a drug."

"Never heard of it."

"It's an old American Indian thing. Helps you pull back the filters, see the world as it really is."

"Sounds cool," she says, her head close to mine on the back of the couch. "And you reckon acid'll do it for you?"

"Well, yeah, maybe."

"You'll see things for sure but I don't know if it's how the world really is. It'd be nice to think it was like that, all the colors. But why the hell would we filter that out?"

"It's probably more about filtering out the bad shit."

"That makes sense. Anyway, shouldn't be long now. A drop of water on that glass there is starting to look solid. What about you? Feel anything?"

I focus on the glass. "A little drunk maybe, but nothing else."

"Don't worry, you won't see your dead mother, or anything. It's not that kind of stuff. It should be all good."

But I don't need it to be *all good*—I want to know what can be found in a sugar cube. I sink into the couch and close my eyes. It won't be long now, I can feel it, the loose shift. One step closer to another world.

Cherry is gazing at her hands. "Wow, look. The veins are so blue."

Mine are spectacular as I turn them, almost transparent. The wall is geometric, every shadow living, but my hands, with their river of veins, exist on another plane.

"Can you see the dragon?" she asks, dancing her fingers over the wall. The dragon, once a shadow, now moves in time with the music, flame-tongued. She whispers, "You are a giant."

I tower above her, the ends of her hair sharp. I touch one of the points.

"Will, what does it mean to be small?"

"Nothing. It means nothing at all."

"Where are you, Will?"

On the table, a bottle, curves of emerald light, the essence of green. It needs to be touched it's so perfect but my fingers won't dare, with their blue veins. I am old. I am many ages at the same time.

Cherry places my hands on the wall. A stain curls, becomes a flower, a spiral. The music heaves its way around her words.

"Will, can you see the flames? They see sky and remember what they are." Her cell phone rings. Something gothic.

"I once imagined my dead body lying on the floor, I sensed the essence of things."

"That's not just incense, Will."

"What?"

"It's music. Music that smells like sandalwood."

"But why can't I push through?" I shiver. "There's no magic here."

"Oh, but there is. Look, flashes of blue light."

I lie on the floor, the smell of beer in the carpet, sweet, putrid, sweet again, my own smell wafting over me. "I am an animal."

"I am too," she says, feeding her fingers through mine. "Will, you need to look at the wall."

"What? The one without a door."

I need to piss; at least I think I do. I go into the kitchen. On the fridge there are magnetic words shaped into sentences and thoughts. The toilet is on the other side, in the bathroom, which is also the laundry, and smells of mold and something bitter. The bowl is marked with dry shit, like tea leaves. Maybe I can read my fortune; surely somewhere in the world there are people who do that. I think I'd better sit to piss because if I don't I'll end up creating some masterpiece on this floor. I lean forward and read my fortune in the bowl between my legs. There's a dark man and a voyage. My stomach doesn't feel so good. I better watch out or all this filth will come home with me. Take up residence in my gut.

I am an animal.

I eat.

I drink.

I shit.

I piss.

I need.

I crave.

I love.

My neck hurts.

"It's the poison," sighs Cherry. "This stuff's never completely clean. Don't worry, it won't last forever. Here, let me massage it."

Hummer comes out rubbing his eyes. It's the first time we've seen him for hours. "How was it?"

"Will's got a sore neck but apart from that it was great, wasn't it, Will?"

"Yeah, I guess. Not quite what I expected."

Hummer grunts. "What, you thought you'd become a ninja turtle?"

"Will was hoping to see God."

"Well, you'll need stronger stuff if that's what you're after." Hummer goes into the kitchen scratching his ass.

"You're disappointed, aren't you?" says Cherry, her tiny fingers working their way into my muscle, relaxing my neck.

"A little. I feel like I need something but I don't know what."

"That's the drugs. They're all about need." She stands up and pulls out a pack of cigarettes. "Sorry you didn't get what you came for. This shit's mainly about having a good time."

"I did," I say, but I know that's not enough, not now.

"You coming?"

"Sure."

"See ya!" she calls out to Hummer, but nothing comes back. We leave the money under the green bottle, the TV illuminating it from behind.

We go out the front door and shade our eyes against the late afternoon light. Cherry stops at the gate. "You want one?" she asks, offering me a cigarette.

I shake my head. "You know, maybe it's all about the wanting," I whisper into the glare.

"Who knows, Will. Come on, let's get out of here." She pulls a pair of sunglasses from her bag.

On the train back home, I flick through my notebook till I find an extract that I tracked down on the Net from *The Doors of Perception*, by that guy who took peyote, Aldous Huxley.

> *The man who comes back through the Door in the Wall will never be quite the same as the man who went out. He will be wiser but less cocksure, happier but less self-satisfied, humbler in acknowledging*

his ignorance yet better equipped to understand the relationship of words to things, of systematic reasoning to the unfathomable Mystery which it tries, forever vainly, to comprehend.

Below it I write:

16: What if the world looks the same on both sides of the Door?

A SMALL DEATH

I ROLL OVER IN BED and remember the flames, the dragon. I keep getting these blue flashes—Cherry said it would happen—the oak outside my window seems almost alive in the morning light, as if it's connected to me. It's nice. Problem is, I don't seem to be making much progress here. But maybe you can't, you just have to hang on when your life goes to shit.

On my bedside table, a quote from Rumi I printed out when I got home last night from Cherry's:

I have lived on the lip of insanity, wanting to know reasons, knocking on a door. It opens. I've been knocking from the inside!

Taryn,

I am so sorry.

♥ Will ♥

Taryn?

I'm here, Will. Just catching my breath.

Sultry night. Today, tomorrow, then exams. I've been trying to study in my room but *Macbeth*'s working on me like a sedative.

The front door bangs open. There's movement in the kitchen so I head down the hall following the light. Dad's got his work pants on but he's only wearing an undershirt. His head's in the fridge. He emerges with a beer in his hand. "Will."

"Hey, Dad."

He fishes around in the drawer for an opener, stabs his finger on something and almost loses his beer.

"Let me do that for you?" I say, taking the bottle from him. He smells of cigarettes and alcohol. "Where've you been? I thought you were at a meeting."

"We went out for a drink afterward."

"Did you get a taxi?" I ask, handing him the open beer.

"No, I drove."

He lifts the bottle up high and takes a swig; some of it bubbles down his chin. I hold up a tea towel but he wipes the beer with the back of his hand. I chuck the tea towel in the sink. "You shouldn't have driven."

"I'm not drunk."

"Bullshit."

Dad looks at me as if I've got the wrong guy. I feel a surge of something like hatred come over me, followed closely by pity and disgust. The sound of the key in the front door. Adam wearing a suit.

"Hey," he says, looking first at me, then at Dad. "Everything all right?"

Dad's peering into his beer. His hair needs a cut.

"He's drunk," I say to Adam, "and he drove home. I'm going to bed." As I walk past Adam, our shoulders connect for a moment and I smell alcohol on him too.

"You okay?" he asks.

I hesitate for a moment but all I say is "Fine."

"Good night, Will."

As I head down the hall, I get a sense of that terrible infinity Nietzsche talked about. Of going it alone. Of having cast off into the great roaring ocean without an anchor. Or even a map.

Memory.

Mom and Dad having a fight. Mom's saying, "Come on, Michael, you're smarter than that." "I know. I'm trying," he says, his head bowed. "They'll kill you," she spits. "At least think of the kids." Between them, a crushed cigarette pack in her fist.

Dad's keys are hanging on the hook where he left them. Both he and Adam are asleep. Let them sleep. I have other things to do tonight.

I move the seat forward—I'm taller than Dad but I like to be close to the wheel; it makes the car feel more like an extension of me. I take the backstreets to avoid traffic. Every white car is like a cop in the rearview mirror, every flash a radar.

All the lights are out at Taryn's house. I drive a little farther and park, no clouds, no darkness to hide me as I walk down Taryn's driveway, around the side of the house, to her room. Her window's open but there's a mosquito screen.

"Taryn."

No movement. I try again. A slow stirring. A light. "Will? Is that you?"

"Yeah. Can I come in?"

"What are you doing here?"

Taryn's at the window, wearing only a tank top. She unclips the screen and I climb in and kiss her on the cheek. "How are you?"

"All right, I guess," she whispers. "How did you get here?"

"I drove."

"What?"

"I took Dad's car."

"Will."

Her hand on my chest. She's still only half-awake.

"I thought you might like to go for a ride with me. We could go up to the mountain and see the city lights."

"What are you talking about?"

"Look, I'm sorry about what happened last Saturday."

"I know, me too. Things are a bit difficult, what with exams and everything. I mean, I know mine aren't as important as yours, but . . ."

"Don't worry about that. Do you want to come?"

"No. I can't believe you took your dad's car."

"I was just sick of . . ."

"Where've you been, Will?"

She's awake now. I know she won't mind about the drugs, not really, but Cherry . . .

"You were with somebody else, weren't you?"

"Not *with*."

"God, Will, I told you, you can tell me anything."

"I know, I'm sorry . . ."

I pull her into me, kiss the top of her head. My mouth works its way down, her temple, her cheek, her lips. She kisses me back, tentatively, and sits on her bed, reaching out for my hand. She notices the cuts.

"You okay?" She frowns and pulls me down on top of her. The air from the ceiling fan feels good across my back. Her bedside lamp lights up the sweat on her skin. Shiny.

"Undress me," she whispers.

So I do, for the first time, my hands sketching her curves. There's desperation in her mouth as she kisses me, and the deeper she goes the more excited I get. I take off my clothes.

"Roll over," I say.

She lies on her stomach and I slip my hand under her hip, pull her up against me. This is the first time we've done it like this and she seems to relax into me but then she drops flat on the bed and turns over.

"Kiss me," she says.

So I do. I press my body against hers, feel the warm of her mouth on mine as I enter her.

"Will."

"It's okay," I whisper, holding on to her shoulders. The perfect rhythm of it. The air whipped by the ceiling fan.

"Will!"

"I'm almost there," I gasp.

She's trying to move out from under me, both hands pressed into my ribs, breath heaving. I roll back. "What's wrong?"

She's sitting huddled in the angle of the wall. "I don't know you anymore."

"What do you mean? Of course you do."

She's shaking her head. I sit back on my feet, tall above her, my hand over my dick. "Maybe this is who I am," I say. I have a disorienting desire to hit out at her and not just with words.

"Then I guess it's lucky I found out now."

And I know in that instant that this could all fall apart. I go to touch her but she moves away, a tear spills down her cheek. "I love you," I say, but it sounds weak as it exits my mouth.

"So you've said, but it's a weird kind of love."

"It's the best I can do right now."

"Well, it's not good enough." She wipes the tear with the back of her hand, dries it on the bed. Her face adjusts. "You need to go now."

I try to think of anything to convince, but I have no arguments. Can't pull out a bit of Plato or Rumi when I need it, as if that will help. As I get up I catch a glimpse of my body in her mirror, the red marks where I rubbed up against her. I must have been pushing her hard. I can't believe I did that. I want to hide myself—what's sex compared to love? I go to say *I love you* again, but now it's worth nothing. I kiss her gently on her forehead.

"Don't, it only makes it worse," she says, pulling away.

"I don't mean to. It's like there's two of me. Things get out of hand."

Another tear falls down her cheek.

"I'm such a shit."

"No, you're not. It would be much easier if you were. But I've got to look after myself."

I notice the beginnings of a bruise on her hip. If only I could rewind a couple of weeks. Even further back than that—before my mother died. But I know I can't. This is where I am now.

As I climb out the window, she raises her hand. Her wave is like a small death.

RITES OF PASSAGE

DAD LEAVES EARLY FOR WORK and doesn't notice anything about the car. Adam skips breakfast. Cherry calls.

She's waiting for me beneath the tunnel, a plastic bag in her hand.

"Check this out," Cherry says, removing a spray can and a book. She opens the book and turns it toward the light slanting in from the end of the tunnel, her finger on a folded page inside, on the line *People living deeply have no fear of death*. "What do you think?"

"Who wrote it?"

"Some French chick called Anaïs Nin. She wrote a lot of erotic stuff."

There's a metallic screech and for a moment I think there's another train coming but there's no telltale wind—must have been a car on the bridge. My quote from Nietzsche is still half-finished on the wall.

"It's good but I'm not really up for this."

"Why not?"

"I feel like shit."

"Come on. Don't be so lame." She's drumming her fingers into my chest, trying to get in under my arm. I grab hold of her hands. "Cherry."

"That's my name. So why did you come then? Did you think I could cheer you up?"

"I don't know."

"I've got something here . . ." She digs around in her bag, and pulls out a small plastic bag. Lined up at the bottom, some white pills.

"It's all right," I say, "I don't need that kind of cheering up."

"Well, what kind do you need?"

I look at her eyes, too fixed on mine, and wonder what she's already taken. I bend down to her face, my body lifting her against the wall as I press into her, her mouth dry and hard, tasting of cigarettes.

"Hey." She turns away from me, her hands against my chest.

"What's wrong? I thought this is what you wanted."

Cherry laughs and shakes her head. "You're such a kid."

"Fuck off."

She staggers, her boot catching on the rail. "Look, forget it. I'm feeling pretty messed up today myself."

She pulls a cigarette out of her bag. I want to ask her what's going on but I can't right now, there's no room.

"Go home, Will. This isn't your kind of place," she says, an echo of Taryn in the words *go home*.

Jigsaw night made up of pieces of sleep. The dawn of my first exam.

* * *

It's the silence that gets you, the blank page, everybody else with their heads down, a few hours to prove yourself worthy. Of what? Passing through to the next stage. As if the proof is finding a few quotes, showing I know how to analyze a text. Is this all I've been doing these last few months? Grabbing a few choice words from philosophers, singers, poets, reading a handful of books, half of which I haven't even finished, like preparing for an exam, no true understanding, just enough to get me through.

But what if I fail?

17. Is it possible to find something to live and die for in words on the page?

Yellow house. Taryn answers the door, wearing a dressing gown.

"Will."

"I wanted to see you."

"Come in."

At her room, I linger by the door, remembering the last time I was here.

"What are you doing here?"

"I had my first exam today."

"I know. And?"

"When I finished I got thinking about what's important."

"Will."

"Do you need some time, is that it?"

She shields her eyes with her hand. "You have no idea."

"But, I do. I've been a shit . . ."

"It's not just that."

"Then, what?"

"I can't tell you, not with exams . . ."

I enter her room. "Forget exams. What is it? Tell me."

"My period's late."

"What?"

"By four days. I'm never late."

"But how?"

She raises her eyebrows at me.

"I mean . . . I thought you were on the pill."

"You know I am, but I was sick a few weeks back. After the party."

"I don't understand. What's that got to do with it?"

"The pill doesn't work properly if you throw up. I read it in the instructions last night. And we didn't use a condom that one time."

She jerks a tissue out of a box by her bed as I remember that day, thinking that there was something about the way we were together that always made me feel we were immune. "Who knows?" I said.

"Nobody yet, except you."

"What are we going to do?"

"Wait. Hope it's a false alarm."

"And if it's not?"

"I don't know, Will."

Taryn leans back on the bed. She buries her face in the duvet, careful not to lean against me. I go to touch her but her body says no. "My parents will be home soon and I don't want them seeing you here. I told them we've stopped going out for a while. There'll be a million questions, and I can't handle that right now."

"But . . ."

"Please, Will."

I put my hand on her head anyway and suddenly she's beside me. "You know I still love you?" she says.

I nod as I realize it's true, for both of us, but if I say the words, they'll hang there, they won't go where they should. "You call me," I say, kissing the top of her head.

18. Can one life replace another?

Nobody's home. Dad's meant to be here, it's his turn to cook. Adam's at some thing. Don't know if I'd tell him anyway. There's nothing to eat in the fridge. Nothing in the cupboard either, except a package of chocolate and peanut cookies and a can of chickpeas. What kind of meal is that? What's happening in this house? Why hasn't Dad done the shopping? Or Adam? I can't be expected to do it, I don't have a license yet, and I've got exams. Anyway, where the hell is he? What kind of father . . . ? Jesus! I can't be responsible for bringing a life into this world when I have no idea about my own. Dad must be working overtime. He said he wouldn't tonight as it's the day of my first exam. Said we could talk about it over dinner. Wonder if it's a boy or a girl? Guess it doesn't make any difference. Will we get rid of it? Does it even exist? I wish Mom was here because I reckon I could tell her, especially since . . . Whoa, that's what I call radical therapy. We finally have the kind of relationship we should've always had. Now that she's dead.

Memory.

My mother's naked body. I'm almost thirteen. She pulls a towel to her chest, says, "It doesn't matter," but it does. Her body seems older than I remember it, less sure of itself, not wanting to be noticed. It has hair on it, a triangle above her legs. I shudder. The place from where I came.

My next exam's not until Tuesday. I need to get the hell out of here. I stick a note to the fridge with a fish magnet: *I'm fine. Don't come looking for me. Will.*

Taryn.

Out beyond ideas of wrongdoing and rightdoing,
there is a field.
I will meet you there.

Rumi

♥ Will

FOUR

MYSTIC ON THE FRINGE

I DON'T REMEMBER THE LAST TIME I took the train out to the end of the line, maybe when I was a kid. The sun's going down, sloping in the window—it's been a long day, and it isn't over yet. In my backpack, a bottle of water, a lighter, a couple of bread rolls I found in the freezer, Mom's camera, my notebook, a shirt, a spare pair of boxers. A book about a French philosopher titled *Foucault for Beginners.* In my pocket, thirty bucks. The train's got a few suits in it, probably heading home after Friday drinks. Maybe that's what happened to Dad. In the next seat, a guy and a girl seriously into each other's tongues. They couldn't give a damn about their audience but all I want to do is to stare down the suburbs as they race past. Try to imagine Taryn being here, but when you're pregnant you can't sleep rough. Pregnant. Shit, that's a big word. Besides, this kind of thing you have to do alone. I read that somewhere but some things you don't need to read about, you know they're true.

The station is lit up. A bunch of kids are waiting to catch the train to the city, making a lot of noise but I can't be bothered looking to see why. I'm hungry but I need to save the two rolls for breakfast. Hope it doesn't rain. The forecast could be wrong. I could also be attacked by a serial rapist or a feral cat. Lucky I brought my coat.

Some of the shops are still open, cheerful lights, clumps of people sitting outside bars. I go into a fish-and-chip shop and order a hamburger. There's nobody I know, don't know why there would be, here on the outskirts. I study my sneakers. I should've worn my hiking boots. Should've, should've, should've.

They call my number and I take my hamburger and sit at one of the round metal tables outside. There are four kids about my age at the next table. One of the guys nods at me. I nod back, watch traffic as I eat. Where do they all go?

The national park's not far up that road. Ten, fifteen minutes' walk. I'll finish this hamburger and then I'll go, make a bed out of branches and leaves. I remember thinking about this stuff when I was a kid, how I'd survive if I got stuck in the bush, what I'd eat. Problem is, I haven't got a clue what will kill me and what will keep me alive. I'd better get some food from the supermarket across the road before I head off. How many mystics went to Safeway before they set off into the wilderness? I guess I'm blazing a new path.

19. How many mystics does it take?

It's night by the time I find the track—I forgot to bring a flashlight and my lighter's not much use. The moon's full but beneath these colossal trees it barely takes the edge off the dark. At least everything's dry. There's nobody around, but there's noise: distant cars, wind in the trees, night sounds. I try to imagine this track during the day, in full sunlight, how it wouldn't threaten at all, but I can't—every rustle, every snap, seems like an omen, a reminder of how I've messed things up.

Everything reduced to one question: where the hell am I going to sleep?

I am lying on my jacket about twenty meters off the track. I put some dry fern on the ground under me—I know it's a national park and you're not meant to pick anything but there seemed to be a lot of stuff moving on the ground, and, well, sometimes necessity outweighs the rules. It's about survival now. I try to calculate how many spiders there would be in a square meter of bush but I know nothing about the mathematics of spiders. The moon is bright above my head, too bright, but at least I can see. I'm about two Ks from civilization but it feels like the rest of the world has slipped into another realm.

Memory.

Family picnic. I'm about four. Dad and Adam are kicking a football around a clearing between the trees and Mom's asleep in the sun. I go exploring, pick my way through parched scrub, the scent of eucalyptus expanding in the heat. I hear a rustle in the leaves and follow it, hoping it's a lizard and not a snake, but I soon lose its track. I can't remember which way I came. I listen out for my family but hear only the sounds of trees. By the time I find my way back to the picnic, nobody's there. I wait, the trees rising higher and higher, till I hear them calling, their voices like invisible bush creatures carried on the wind. I stare at the impression of my mother's body in the grass.

* * *

Warm fog: 6:30 a.m.

After a five o'clock wake-up, I burned leeches off my leg, singed some hair while I was doing it, and ate my two rolls. Finished half of my water. Then I heard people go past on the nearby path and hunted down a couple more leeches and burned them off.

This is not what I expected, but, considering the sum total of five minutes I spent thinking about it before leaving, I shouldn't be surprised. One should plan for spiritual enlightenment. At least bring a flashlight.

I'm still hungry, but only because I have a finite amount of food in my bag. Maybe I can find something to eat in the bush. The Aborigines ate berries but I can't see any around here. Maybe they preferred possum; I heard enough of those last night, like chain saws, screaming in the dark.

A woman with long gray hair comes striding down the track. She looks about Mom's age, maybe older, magpie eyes, a dried leaf stuck in her hair.

"Hello," she says.

"Hi."

I pull my backpack higher on my shoulder as she points to a bush in front of me. "That's *coprosma quadrifida*. Prickly currant bush. You here alone?"

"I'm just going for a walk."

"You're not lost, are you?" she asks, looking at my sneakers.

"No."

"Well, be careful. You never know who you might run across out here." She taps her walking stick on the ground, hesitates a moment, before marching off down the track, not bothering to dodge a patch of mud.

There are too many people in this forest. I tuck my jeans into my socks and look for a break in the trees. There's a gap between two giant gums that could be a path. I head for it. It's quite open except I have to climb over logs to follow it, and there are big holes, probably from wombats. The ground is littered with bark. My foot snags and I trip, fly headfirst toward a log, which I somehow avoid and land hard on my shoulder instead. I lie still, my face in a pile of eucalyptus leaves. I can hear the sound of cockatoos, wind, the creak of giant trees. I sit up and flex my shoulder, stretch the neck of my T-shirt to take a look at it, stripes of blood lined up against the white of the graze. That bark is lethal.

The track heads down steeply. I have to hold on to trees, steady my feet against roots. The last of the Band-Aids tears off my knuckle, making it bleed again. A couple of times there seem to be two possible directions, so I go with instinct. I can hear the trickle of water, probably a creek. I follow the sound. The bush becomes denser, somber—ferns reach around each other, lean into rocks, the ground springy, water dangling from tiny moss fronds. The smell of rotting and things growing.

The creek keeps disappearing under shelves of moss but I follow it upward, trying not to touch anything as I make my way. This place is primeval; there are hardly even any birds, no screeching cockatoos. They don't belong here. It's hard to stay close to the creek, it's so overgrown, fallen logs trapped between rocks as I climb a ridge, my shoulder aching, and work my way back down. Up ahead, a rock face, though it looks more like the wall to a dam. So much for the lost world.

I scramble around the side of it, grab hold of roots and branches and haul myself up. Barely visible through the trees, there's a small jade lake sitting in the sun. Pitched beside it, a domed gray tent.

* * *

Memory.

Camping by a river. Mom hates camping so she usually doesn't come, but this time she decides to join *the boys*. Dad and Adam have gone looking for wood. I'm staring at the river, how fast it's moving. I spy a tiny blue wren tracking me as it jumps from branch to branch. I edge toward it, remembering what Mom taught me about how to get close to a bird. With the mind of a cat. I get close but at the last minute it darts away. By the river's edge, the sun is hot on my feet—I want to dip them in the water, to see how cold it is. I stick one toe in, then my whole foot, the sand slipping beneath me, the river strong, my body following my feet. A shout and a pain around my throat. It's Mom, she's got me by my T-shirt and she's dragging me out, yelling at me for going so close to the edge. Her arms wrapped around me, so tight I can hardly breathe.

I can't see anybody around. The lake's small, maybe thirty meters wide, completely overgrown around the edges, hard to tell how deep. Overhead, a pair of rosellas dip their way across the sky as a guy walks out of the trees at the far side of the tent.

"Hello," I say. He walks toward me, drops something by his tent as he goes past. He's bald, and tall, and coming for me. I step back.

"Saul," he says, wiping his hand on his trousers and holding it out. I hesitate before shaking it. His grip is strong. Something moves in the bush. "Sssshhh," he says, crouching down.

I squat too, follow his eyes to see what would make such a solid guy go for cover. He's wearing a khaki shirt with dirt on one shoulder and there's a shadow where his hair would be if he let it grow. Another rustle. Below us in the bush is a large brown bird. I smile.

"It's a lyrebird," he whispers.

"I thought lyrebirds had big tail feathers."

"That's a female." He cocks his head to the side as she moves through the bush. She scratches at the ground with her feet, looking for food, and makes a noise like a cockatoo. Saul turns to me, his face too close. "Hear that? Great imitators, lyrebirds. She can copy any bird in the bush, even do a good version of a chain saw."

"What is this place?" I ask, as the lyrebird moves away and we both stand up.

"People call it *the secret lake*."

"Not very original."

"I guess not. I shouldn't be camping here, but you won't turn me in, will you?"

He raises his eyebrows, the only hair on his head, but I can't tell whether he's making fun of me or not. I go over to the edge of the lake. The water's tea-colored from above, not jade, its surface stagnant, littered with leaves and a white feather.

"I come here sometimes, to get away. Nobody knows I'm here." He pulls up the bottom of his trousers and starts checking his legs. They have no hair either.

"Looking for leeches?"

"Yeah, little bastards. I've got some salt."

"Burned mine off with my lighter."

"Did you sleep in the bush last night?"

"Yeah."

"Any particular reason?"

"Yeah."

"You always this talkative?"

"No, I'm usually the silent type."

"What's your name?" he asks, rolling down his trousers.

"Will. So, what do you do up here?"

"Think."

"About what?"

"Oh, you know, the meaning of life as we know it, what it's all about." He laughs. "Monty Python fan from way back. I take off once a year for a week," he says, undoing the fly on his tent.

"You always come here?"

"Sometimes. I've got a few spots. I'm a computer programmer," he says, as if that explains everything. Maybe it does.

"My mother died."

Saul squats by the open fly, his back to me, and pulls out a plastic tub. "I've got some tea. Would you like some? It's already got the milk mixed in. I wasn't expecting company."

"Yeah, all right."

He hands me a cupful and pours some into the lid of the thermos for himself. "So, how did she die?"

"Got hit by a drunk driver getting out of her car. She was going to a doctor's appointment."

"When?"

"Nine weeks and two days ago."

He stares at me for a moment, his forehead creased with parallel lines. "Does anybody know where you are?"

I have no idea who this man is, he could be a psycho. I'm sure plenty of computer programmers are half-mad. Maybe he's not even a programmer. "I left a message saying where I was. I'm going back tomorrow night."

"You can stay here if you like, I've got plenty of food."

"Maybe."

He points up the hill to a patch of sun among the trees. "I'll be up there if you need me. I've found a good spot to do some reading. If you decide not to stay, it was nice meeting you, Will."

He pulls a book that looks like a novel out of a bag in his tent, and heads off into the bush.

A ripple spreads out from the middle of the lake.

What I write in my notebook by the water's edge:

[1]
You can't see the wind but you can
see what it does, its movement
through leaves and grass. Like the
larva that's dangling in front of me
by an invisible thread.
I know it's there, that thread, even
though I can't see it—logic tells me it
is. Or is it a question of faith? In
science? In the way the world's
supposed to be?

[2]
Ants work around me on the log.
When you squash them they smell
like piss. Do they think I have an
agenda or a purpose?
Am I good or evil according to the
philosophy of ants? Or are they just
waiting till I die, so they can pick me
to the bone?

[3]
A fallen log covered in moss.
The living grow around the dead
in order to survive.

[4]
All things reach for their
piece of the sun.

[5]
Why, in nature, does everything
become a metaphor?

CHAOS THEORY

THERE IS NOTHING to do here except eat, drink, sleep, think, forget. I have that book in my bag but I don't feel like taking it out—there are already enough ideas fighting for space in my head. I'm going to sit here among the ferns till I can make sense of it all. Lucky I've got the whole afternoon. The lake is still, except it only seems that way—there is constant movement, the flow of the water, slow, subtle, carrying everything with it, feathers, debris, leaves. Water trickles in one end and out the other. I take a deep breath and let it go, listen to the hum of insects in tune with the cadence of my heart, and close my eyes. A gentle emptying. The color blue. And a feeling a lot like love.

The shriek of a bird.

I open my eyes. A dragonfly comes to rest on a stick near my foot. There have been many great thinkers, but, in the end, they were all just seeking their own truth. I can do that, can't I, by the side of a lake?

Saul invites me for lunch and I decide I might as well. We have cans of tuna and an apple, with some more tea, and cookies for dessert. The cookies are mine but everything else is Saul's. Then Saul tells me his story, because I asked.

Saul's Story

His dad was a bus driver, his mom worked part-time, making hats. He had two brothers and one sister—one of his brothers died in a boating accident when Saul was sixteen. When he was young, his favorite band was The Who but he never took drugs and he only had sex once before he got married. Her name was Sue, and it wasn't what he'd expected. At university he studied engineering because he liked answers, but he gambled, especially with cards.

Two days after his first child was born, he was sitting at home after visiting his wife in the hospital, and he suddenly realized he had no idea who he was. It went away when the baby got home because all that mattered was getting enough sleep, but it came back again about a year later, when he got a promotion. At the exact moment when his boss shook his hand, into his head leaped the question Is this all there is? *So, he started going away for a day or two into the bush, taking with him a bag full of books. A tent. His thermos. His brother's sleeping bag he'd inherited when he died.*

He reads all sorts of philosophy. He has his favorite philosophers, though sometimes they change. He remembers sitting next to a hunched tree fern on the other side of the lake, reading about Jean-Paul Sartre's idea of bad faith, *how people lie to themselves about their lives, and that the sun came out and lit up drops of water hanging from moss fronds on the fern. He will never forget that moment as long as he lives.*

On Sunday afternoons he listens to opera turned up loud if nobody's home. He has never smoked a cigarette in his life.

I decide to stay for the night.

I chop up onions and chili peppers for Saul while he gets his gas cooker going, and a couple of times I almost cut myself the knife's so blunt. Around the lake, the birds are swooping and plunging for insects as the sun goes down.

"Best time of the day," says Saul, "if you don't count dawn."

He opens a box of couscous and pours some into a bowl. He has big fingers, more like you'd expect on a builder than a programmer. In fact, he doesn't look like a programmer at all.

"Do you do a lot of sports, Saul?"

"Yeah, actually, I swim a bit, and cycle, and I still play rugby." He grins. "On an old guys' team."

"You any good?"

"Used to be, though now it's just for fun. I like a drink with the guys after a game, bit of barroom philosophizing."

"Do you tell them about this?"

"No."

I scrape the onions into the frying pan; they spit as they hit the oil. "Do you think it helps, reading all that philosophy?"

"Depends what you mean by *help*. It gives you clarity. And, there's always the companionship."

I go to ask him what he means by that, but then I realize. A familiar voice in the dark.

I live in a nice house. My family aren't that bad, they even love me, but here I am, in the middle of a rain forest, with a man I hardly know—a man who smells like onions, and farts in his sleep. He offered for me to sleep in the tent but I said no. Instead I'm battling it out on my bed of ferns, surrounded by mosquitos, by the edge of the lake. Wonder if Taryn's awake, if she's afraid? She looked it yesterday afternoon, curled up all fetal on her bed, but so full of love. She's taught me that I'm able to love, too.

I pull the blanket Saul lent me over my head and hear him roll over in the tent. How did it all get so complicated? I want to break things down into a simple equation—nine weeks and two days ago my mother died, four days later I fell in love. I have taken twelve rolls of film with my mother's camera. I have four exams to go. Taryn and I have slept together thirteen times. Somebody dies, you fall in love, you have sex, a new life is created. Is that the formula for life?

Above me, a cluster of stars is visible through the trees. A constellation I recognize, not from a book, but a face.

Dream.

My mother floating in a lake, face to the moon. Her hair is long and fanned out around her head, her body white. I want to touch her. I try to call her name but she doesn't hear; nothing comes out of my mouth. The water is dark but the moon makes a path of light across the lake that reaches to my feet. As I watch her, my mother turns her head to me, her face serene. I step out onto the water and walk toward my mother. I am almost with her, not far now. And when I reach her, I know she will show me that beneath the water it is possible to breathe.

SLEEPWALKING

THE FIRST THING I SEE when I open my eyes is the mist off the water, birds slicing through it, their paths visible as it shifts.

I need some breakfast. Over by the tent, Saul's already got the cooker going. I stretch my legs under the blanket, feel the stiffness of them, the ferns flat beneath my body.

"Morning. How were the mosquitoes?"

"Vicious," I say, scratching my cheek. I go over to my pack. Inside there's a squashed baguette that looks as if it's been used to beat off a mad bull.

"I've got some muesli," Saul says. "What else have you got in there?"

I pull out a bag of mini chocolate bars, two bananas, an apple, and a can of baked beans. The copy of *Foucault for Beginners* with a cartoon of a guy wearing glasses on the front.

"Bit of light reading, huh?" Saul opens the package of muesli and pours some into a bowl, some into the cup he's been lending me. My all-purpose cup. A finch flits in a fern tree next to the tent, the light through the fronds reminding me of that green bottle, doing acid, being with Cherry. Taryn's eyes.

"So, tell me more about Sartre. This woman I met on a bus talked about him."

"A lot of stories start with somebody on a bus." Saul points his spoon at me. "When I first read Sartre I remember thinking, isn't it comforting that all this is random? That no God, no force, created this mess on purpose."

"I guess."

"And why should I feel anxious about my own nonexistence? Do I get all worked up when the mist on the lake disappears? My life only has value because I give it value. If I realize this, really believe it in my gut"—Saul slaps himself on the stomach—"then there can be no anxiety. Anxiety is an illogical response to the meaninglessness of life."

"Are you always like this over breakfast?"

"No." He laughs. "My family would run a mile. So what do you think?"

I steady myself on my log—I'm not perfectly balanced and it takes a bit of effort not to fall off. "Makes you feel a bit stupid."

"Why?"

"For ever worrying about anything at all."

"Sure. But then we do have to live in the world and give meaning to things."

I think of Mom, Taryn, her face when she kisses me. Things I know about love.

He looks up at me. "For example, it makes no sense to love someone who will die, but no matter how much we try, we still cling to the thing that suggests meaning. In the end, it's all about finding a way to live."

"Oh, well that's easy."

Saul puts his bowl on the ground. Ants climb into the leftover milk. The finch is still hanging around. "That's why I come here. Keep the bullshit detector running, and once a year take stock, question whether I'm living blindly, following the pack. Heidegger got me onto that."

"Never heard of him," I say, moving over to the edge of the lake.

"Of course, I still mess up," he laughs, "but once you start living authentically it's like waking up from a long sleep. If you see a lot of people as sleepwalkers, it helps you understand why they act like they do."

There's an arrogance in what he's saying that makes me shift on my feet. "You seem pretty sure of yourself."

"I've given it a bit of thought. Look, we all enjoy deception, it's a comfortable way to be, but, in the end, is it really? Aren't there always little voices saying, You're kidding yourself, there's more to life than this"?

His theory sounds like *less* rather than *more*. "My little voices have escalated to a shout lately."

"A death will do that." He looks sideways at me. "To some."

I've had about enough of his bullshit. "What's that supposed to mean?"

"Just that some people take things harder than others."

God, he's so brutal. If he's so sure of himself, why's he still going bush to work it all out? Isn't he a bit old for that? "Yeah, well, maybe some of us have a heart."

He doesn't call after me as I go up the hill to a place in the sun dwarfed by the trees. As I flop in a nest of bark far from the tent, a fly goes past, twice, three times, almost smacks into my head, the sound it makes disproportionate to its size, and I know if it crosses me again I'll catch it. Squash the little bastard so flat he'll wish he'd never even been a thought.

Saul is so frigging logical. I remember Taryn saying that about me once. I can follow it, his line of reasoning, that there is only the significance we give to things. That nothing has any built-in meaning that can't be argued away. Not even love. All is empty, that's what the Buddhists would say, and I guess you have two options: Western anxiety or Eastern bliss. Nice thought. If only it were a matter of choice.

I've been anxious, there's no doubt about that, so crushingly anxious that sometimes I can barely breathe, unlike Saul. But I bet he's probably as scared as anybody else. Bet if he found out he had cancer his theories would fold before his speculating eyes.

Below, the lake is deceptively still. I try to imagine it as a pool of wisdom, but I know there's no wading around the edges, not for me. I'd have to dive in, sink or swim. That's my way. And this lake could swallow me up, I could be consumed by ideas, other people's, my own, one more drop in the thought ocean, swirling around with all the others.

The lake shimmers and grows, is all around me. I am it. I am the trees that lean into its depths, the sunlight on its surface, but it's not beautiful, like what Huxley saw when he was on drugs, and it's not frightening, it just is. I focus on a bright green leaf, rotating, the flash of a blue wren, Saul sitting by his tent. But I am alone, again. I will die alone and I see it before me like a great endless falling.

Was it like that for Mom?

God, I miss her. I feel it in my gut, a rip, a tearing in half as I drop, steady myself against the ground, and throw up everything, my ribs coiling with the violence of it, until all that's left are long strings of spit and this retching that won't give up. She's not coming back. Ever. Nothing I say or do or read can change that. But she is close now, I sense her, closer than she's been since her death, maybe more than in life.

The retching turns to shaking. I'm so cold. And then it rises up from inside me, as if it's being pulled out by a rope, a great unraveling, a snake leaching my guts, and I start to cough, the blood banging away inside my head. I see the small, shut-off boy in me, standing by her graveside, and I begin to sob, my hands ripping at the dirt, at leaves. I scratch a fragment of green glass that looks like part of the neck of a bottle. I pull the shard loose and hold it up to the light. Its edge is worn but I know it will cut if I ask it to.

I am still now. A dead leaf lands beside my knee.

I press the glass against my wrist. A drop of blood travels along the edge and slips to the ground. I admire the shine of it, the red of plums. It's all about metering out the pain. I know how this works. A little deeper, millimeters, that's all it takes, like the stopping up of breath.

The drops multiply and unite. I notice the pain now, but it is confined to my wrist. It's not like grief. There's something cheap about it. This is my blood, my life, but as I watch it soak into the ground, I know that all I want is to remember how to live.

Memory.

Me, coming in the front door after school, Mom standing in front of the hall mirror, her hand on her left breast. As she turns toward me, I see fear in her face. A tear runs the length of her cheek. It is one week before her death.

I scramble down the bank and hurl the piece of glass into the lake, dip my wrist in the dark water and rinse the sleeve of my shirt. The blood leaves a gray stain. There are bits of spew on my sneakers, which I clean off with leaves, but I can't get rid of the smell. My ribs ache and the sun is warm on my spine. I check my wrist but the blood is already starting to congeal. A bird skims across the surface of the lake.

I make my way through the bush back to the tent, my legs still a bit shaky. Saul's frowning as I come down. "You okay?"

He must've heard me up there losing it, and for a second I almost confess what happened, but he's not the right person to tell. "I'm fine."

"Listen, I'm sorry . . ."

"Don't worry about it."

His eyes fall on my wrist poking out from under my wet sleeve. "You sure you're okay?"

"Yes, but I should be getting home."

"Know how to find your way back?"

"Think so. I'm usually okay with that kind of thing."

"It's been good having you here," he says without looking up. "Listen, there's something I wanted to tell you about. It might help."

I shove my camera into my pack. I'm not much in the mood for advice, especially not from Saul.

"Once a year I write a letter that I never send. My wife knows about it, I keep it propped against my computer screen. She doesn't know what's in it, only to open it if I die."

"Look, I should get going." Saul holds out his hand. I shake it, feel those strong fingers around my thin hand, the one I haven't quite grown into. "Saul. Do you think . . . ?"

"What?"

"Do you think we were meant to meet?"

"Sorry, don't believe in that kind of thing."

I nod. "Thanks for the food, anyway."

"No problem. You've got my email address?"

As I pat my bag he rests his hand on my shoulder. "That letter I mentioned—it contains a list of who and what is important in my life."

I smile. Beside us is a lyrebird, maybe the same one, but this time it's imitating a different sound. A kookaburra's laugh.

The path is open before me, the air is clear. I need to run, to be a body moving fast through the world, wind in my face, heart beating in my ear. I want to spread my fingers till the skin begins to crack, throw my face to the sky and, in the presence of giants, shed my old self like a snake.

LEAP

ON THE TRAIN THERE ARE LOTS OF PEOPLE, seventeen down at my end of the car. The sound of metal, my body being rocked from side to side. I need to call Taryn as soon as I get home.

I open my notebook to where I started writing when Mom died. First up, the quote from *Macbeth*, followed by the questions one after the other, right up to *How many mystics does it take?* Sounds like a lightbulb joke. There's the list of aphorisms I wrote by the lake, photos glued in, a succession of notes and thoughts. The napkin with Taryn's line, *Run naked through your fears.*

And scattered around all of it are the quotes from philosophers, and a lot more poets than I would have thought. They seem split down the middle between the idea of a single truth—the same one for everybody—or a whole lot of individual truths. But which is it? So much of what is written here sounds right, small scraps of what could be true.

I flick back to the questions. There are nineteen of them, but in the game we played when we were kids, it was always twenty questions to work out the identity of a thing. Animal, mineral, vegetable. Beneath my list is a quote from Wittgenstein: *If a question can be framed at all, it is also possible to answer it.* What will my twentieth question be?

The train passes close to the cemetery. Eight stations to go till mine.

Adam's leaning over the kitchen counter, the bones of his shoulders fist-shaped beneath his skin. He turns around as I come in. "You've got a nerve. Dad's been shitting himself."

"Hi, Adam," I say, putting down my pack.

He glares at me and lowers his voice. "Don't go waking Dad, he's having a rest. He's hardly slept the last two nights."

"I left a note."

"Hell of a lot of use that was."

"I'm fine, okay? Look, I have to call . . ."

"You're fine, but what about Dad?" Adam grabs my arm as I go past. I don't try to pull free. "You could've called him."

"You didn't when you didn't come home for two days. Anyway, there weren't any phones where I was."

"And where was that, then?" he asks, letting me go.

"I was up in the bush. I met this guy by a lake. His name's Saul."

"What do I care what his name is? I've had Dad upset all weekend, going crazy. I couldn't leave him on his own. So what the hell were you doing up there anyway? Finding yourself?"

Same old Adam, and we're doing the same old thing, but this time I don't take the bait. "I needed some time to think."

"Was that Samara's idea? Do a bit of meditating in the bush? I ran into her last week and she told me she'd been teaching you how."

"Just the once. I wasn't very good at it."

"So . . ." His body eases.

"Will?"

"Dad."

He's scratching his head, his shirt hanging out of his trousers. "When . . . ?"

"A few minutes ago. Sorry we woke you."

"I'm just glad . . ." Outside, a bird taps at the window but Dad remains still. "I've been absent. I've been absent since your mother died, even before that, but worse since."

"I'm sorry you were worried. I needed . . ."

Adam grunts, his jaw set. "God, Will, not everything's about you."

"You're right, it's not. It's about all of us and how much this fucking hurts." Dad flinches. "And what are you so angry about, anyway? You've been a shit ever since you arrived."

"That's not true."

"It is," says Dad, his eyes tired. "More or less."

Adam glares at me and seems taller than me even though he's not.

"What?" I ask.

For a moment his face opens before shutting down again. Dad's the first one to speak. "Adam, Will asked you a question."

"Forget it," he says, rushing past me, nearly knocking Dad over on his way through. I call after him but he's already gone.

"What was that all about?" I ask Dad, but as I do, I remember things, a thousand small details, an inventory of looks and words.

"He always was a bit jealous of you, the way you were with your mom."

"That's not my fault."

"It's nothing to do with whose fault any of this is. Was it you who took her camera?" Dad's eyes are more focused than they've been for ages.

"I didn't think you'd noticed."

"You've been in our room a couple of times from what I've seen. But it's okay, I don't mind. I think it's good that you find ways of dealing with all this. God knows, it's the hardest thing I've ever had to do. So, have you taken any photos?"

"Yeah, I have, actually."

"Can I see them?"

"Now?"

"Yes, please." Dad sits at the table and tucks in his shirt. The hair is still thick and dark on the top of his head except for a single streak of gray that I never noticed before tonight.

"I'll go and get them."

There's no sign of Adam. From under my bed, I draw out my wooden box, remove the envelopes full of photos I had developed, all twelve rolls of them, plus one extra. The last images Mom ever took.

Adam's waiting for me in the hall, pinching at his bottom lip. "When you were born, I felt I lost her, lost something. Does that sound weird?"

"No, not at all."

"I think all of this kind of reminded me of that."

I want to touch him, but for now words are good. "You okay?"

"Sure."

For the first time in a long time, maybe ever, I feel I can ask him anything, and he won't mind. "What do you miss most about her?"

Adam runs his fingers through his hair. "The way she could always let you know that she loved you."

"Yeah."

"I'm sorry, Will."

His hand goes to my shoulder and he pulls me in, his arms tight around my chest as I feel my body relax. His too. When he releases me, his jaw looks even more like Mom's in the half-light of the hall.

Memory.

Two days before she died. I'm watching TV in the living room on my own. The woman on the show is giving birth but it's not going well—it looks like she might lose the baby, monitors beeping, tubes like tentacles, blood everywhere. I feel a hand on my shoulder. It's Mom. People tangoing in and out of emergency, the dread in the woman's eyes, a scream. The baby held up to the woman's face, a kiss, a simple act of love. My mother's hand.

Dad smiles and I spread the photos out till they cover the whole surface of the table. I curl the strap around the camera and place it beside them. Dad sifts through them, holds up the one of my mother's dress to take a closer look. "You know, she wanted to go to the Himalayas and take pictures. That was before she got pregnant. We never went."

Adam pulls out the photo of the word *DEATH* written into concrete. It was partly hidden under a picture of a wing. "They're good. What are they for?"

"They're a record."

"Of what?"

Dad rests his finger on a photo of a dead bird. "A life. At least the part since your mom died." He looks up at me. "I didn't think you were coming back. God, I was so worried. You hear about it, boys doing themselves in."

"I would never . . ." I begin, but I think of the piece of green glass, and the rest of my words dissolve into doubt. In front of me, my brother and my father, the photos, a mosaic of grief. There are so many things I could quote that might make Dad feel better. Some of them might even be close to the truth. All those things that I've thought, read, experienced, since she died. But how do you roll all that up in a sentence, how do you make it count?

"I miss her," he says.

For a moment it's as if she's there with us, that we're intact again, but when Dad stacks the photos, we return to a triangle of men.

"You should put these in an album, Will."

"Yeah, I might. Not sure what I want to do with them. I'm not quite finished yet."

"She would've wanted you to have the camera. Which reminds me, there's something I want to show you both. I'll be right back."

When he has gone, Adam points to the only envelope I didn't open. "What are those?"

"They were in the camera when Mom died."

He flips through the images—Dad leaning against a tree, a white feather, us at the mountains, me with long hair. He holds the last one up. "This was when I found you standing too close to the edge of the cliff. I remember your face. How strange," he says, his voice steady. "She was there and she didn't say anything. She'd always been so protective, but there she let you . . ."

I take another look at the photo, my face shaped by vertigo, an expression so familiar in the mirror since she died.

"You know, I thought I could protect you," he says, "protect you from what happened. But I couldn't even protect myself."

Dad walks in. He's holding a piece of white paper which he gives to Adam.

"What's this?"

"It's a poem I found in her things. Going by the date, she wrote it soon after you were born."

Adam unfolds the page and reads:

half moon—
my son laughs
and I am whole again

Dad sleeps in clean sheets. Tonight he changed them for the first time since Mom died. Adam dreams of childhood days at the beach. The house is thick with grief, but there are doors and windows. My bed feels good after sleeping on the ground.

THE DIVINITY OF LOVE

MEMORY.

A missing shoe. Mom's late for work, again. Dad's already left. "The cork ones," she says, as if I know what that means, and runs out of the room. Before I can shake my head, she's back again, "You know which pair I mean?" "No idea," I say, putting an apple in my bag. She doesn't find the shoe, has to change her trousers, wear boots instead. She dies that afternoon. I never eat that apple. Two weeks later I find a shoe under the couch. It has a piece of chewing gum stuck to the heel. The heel is made of cork.

I know where she is but I go down to the old part of the cemetery first and check out the names of the dead, where they come from—Sarona, Haifa—places I've never heard of, but now they rest here.

Mom's stone is in the new part. It's shiny black with rough-cut edges. Somebody's left flowers. Chrysanthemums. I don't know whether to sit or stand, the space is so open. Nobody else is around except for some men off in the distance, digging a new grave.

I squat on the concrete next to her headstone. It's been raining, so it's damp and the grass is growing back where her body was laid. She's down there, what's left of her; the coffin was varnished so it must be still intact. Her body. What happens to a body that's been buried for two months? I'd like to know. Some part of me is in love with the facts.

"Mom?"

No one can hear me, the gravediggers are too far away, and the only sounds are birds, the eternal hum of traffic, wind tearing at the trees. I remove a leaf that's got stuck to the stone in the rain and lean in. "Mom? I'm okay. You'd be proud of me, I've learned how to cook. And I've got a girlfriend. Her name's Taryn." The concrete's cold under my ass. I shift. "Her period's late."

Taryn didn't call back last night after I left a message. I wish I knew why. It begins to rain, so I pull the hood up on my jacket and draw the cord tight. "I've been using your camera. I knew you wouldn't mind. My photos are different from yours, but I think I know why. Anyway, it helps."

A lady with greyhounds walks along the other side of the fence, which reminds me of an old joke about cemeteries, but I can't quite remember how it goes. Mom would, she loved sick jokes. I want to call her Anna. "Remember when I had a thing about calling you by your first name, and you said, *There are only two people in the world who can call me Mom*. But, now that you're dead . . ."

The word seems absurd. "Anna," I say, sheltering in on myself, and it's like she's with me again, in the folds of my jacket, all sorts of Annas: the one from the photo with Dad, a vague smell I can remember, oranges, diving into surf. "I've been remembering things. There was something wrong with you, wasn't there?

That's why you were going to the doctor's. You thought you were going to die, but not the way you did. Why didn't you tell us?"

The rain stops again suddenly and the sun comes out and starts evaporating the drops on the concrete. It has a bit of help from the wind.

"I've also been thinking about whether there might be a God," I say, my breath warm inside my jacket. "You could give me some insights into that."

I smile and remember a line from Wittgenstein—*If a lion could talk, we could not understand him*. If the dead could speak, would we understand them?

"Maybe it's because now I get what it might be like to feel a presence. Is it you, or something to do with being in love?"

The gravediggers are taking a break among the headstones; they must see plenty of people confessing to the dead. "On this show I watched, they said we're hardwired to believe in something that's not there."

I raise my head out of my jacket. What I'm hoping for right now is a sign—a ray of light, some voice in my head. I have this desire in me for something beyond logic. I need to believe. Or maybe what I want is for a book with all the answers to land at my feet. *The Book of Everything*. Except, I don't. Not unless it's got a few blank pages in it where I can write all about this. My chapter. Life according to Will.

"I miss you," I whisper, and for a moment the sun illuminates the stone, before the clouds close again.

The Book of Everything.
Part One: What it is to die.
Part Two: What it is to live.

The light drops and it starts to rain really hard. My jacket's waterproof but my jeans are getting soaked. I'm cold. Water trickles down my neck.

"Will?"

I follow the voice from the fresh grass to the dark, wet hems of jeans. Green jacket. Taryn's tall beneath an umbrella, large drips gathering on one of its spikes and falling onto my knee. I'm so glad to see her but I don't feel quite ready.

"Adam said you'd be here." Taryn crouches beside me. She puts her hand on my drenched knee. "You okay, Will?"

"I'm fine. What about you?"

"I'm not pregnant."

"Are you sure?"

"Yes."

I go to say *good*, but it feels like the wrong word. She rests the stem of the umbrella against her shoulder, sheltering both of us. I slide my arm around her, smell the incense and her damp hair. Her fingers weave a pattern on my knee. Circles. Small ones. A drop of water quivers on the scar above her lip. "Did you want to be pregnant?"

"No, not really." She looks down at our hands as I thread my fingers through hers. "Though a part of me did. Something to do with love."

She leans into my chest. I go to say her name out loud but instead I hold it in my head and try to make it fit the body pressing into mine. I have been inside her, tasted her bare skin. I know the sound of desire in her throat, the way she lets slip a small laugh when she's not quite sure. She has let me cross the threshold into her world. Part of me is hers.

She takes my hand and draws it around her, so tight I can

feel my arm beginning to constrict her breath. The fact that I love her makes it possible to exist.

Taryn allows the umbrella to drift to the ground. "Anna," she says, reading the inscription.

I go to tell her things about my mother, but I'm not sure where to begin. Taryn digs around in her pocket and pulls out a small gray stone. She places it on the top of the grave before passing another to me. I steady my hand and balance my stone on top of hers. I touch her cheek. "I might never have met you if she hadn't died."

"Is that okay?"

"Of course it is. I'm sorry," I hear myself saying. "I've done things . . ."

"It was a really hard time for you . . ."

"Still."

"Still," she nods, her lips grazing my cheek.

I lift the umbrella above our heads.

As we walk toward the station, I look back at my mother's grave, the two stones balanced one upon the other, and picture what is written there, the words illegible through the rain. Dad must have chosen them—I didn't notice at the funeral, not until today. Carved in white letters into the smooth black stone are the words *To live on in the hearts of those we love is not to die.*

20. What fragment of truth will be mine?

Memory.

My mother in a long white dress and pearl earrings. Beautiful. I gaze up at her and ask her if she's an angel, but she smiles and says, “I’m going to a party.” She’s dusting powder on her face. “What is it?” she asks, seeing me still there. I reach out, touch that lovely white dress with my fingers, “When are you going to die?”

“Not for a long time,” she says, kissing me on the cheek.

ACKNOWLEDGMENTS

I wish to thank Catherine Clift for embracing Will's story from the outset, and Josh Overs, who was younger than Will when this all began, for his insight and unrelenting honesty. Also, Tom Joyce, Cath Tregillis, Simon Palfrey, Robert Hillman, Marian Spires, and Donna Jordan, for listening, reading and responding, each in their own way. I see you all in quiet corners of this story.

Penny Hueston of Text Publishing in Australia, with her meticulous eye for detail, helped shape this novel from its raw beginnings to what it has become. To Penny, and to Michael Heyward for his part in this, my gratitude is unbounded. My thanks also to Anne Beilby for helping me find a readership overseas, and to Kirsty Wilson, my publicist, for her professionalism and generosity of spirit.

Since the release of my novel in Australia and New Zealand, I have received many wonderful responses from readers and want to thank them for their openness and enthusiasm for my work.

One morning, not so long ago, I received a very exciting call from New York—it was from Margaret Ferguson, Editorial Director at Farrar Straus Giroux Books for Young Readers, telling me how much she loved my novel and wanted to publish it. I am looking forward to taking Will's story to a new audience.

Finally, a special thank you to my boys, without whom none of this would make any sense.